Jeremiah had never wanted to kiss any woman so badly in his life.

Knowing there might never be another opportunity with her—not with a child involved—he decided to live for *this* moment.

He leaned toward Ally, who only had time to suck in a stunned breath before he pressed his mouth against hers, fully.

Softly.

What was so different about this woman that kept him making a fool of himself and coming back for more?

She wanted him. No matter what she did, how remote and disinterested she seemed, this kiss wasn't lying.

Before he changed his mind, he took up his hat, put it on his head, then stood.

"'Night, Ally," he said.

Jeremiah sauntered to his truck, wondering how the hell he was going to stay away from Ally Gale now.

Dear Reader,

Welcome to the second book in the Billionaire Cowboys, Inc., miniseries!

I wanted to write about a family who's undergoing a crisis, and if the first story was the immediate fallout after an emotional explosion, this second book is about the lasting devastation that can result unless our hero can be saved.

Fortunately, he finds the perfect woman to heal him. Unfortunately, she's his polar opposite—a good girl to his bad boy. Is she strong enough to tame this tycoon playboy? I hope you have fun discovering the answer.

The miniseries will conclude with the third book, which will be Chet's story, so look out for that soon, as well!

If you'd like to find out more about my work, come on over to www.crystal-green.com, where I've got contests, a blog and updated news. Meanwhile, happy reading!

All the best,

Crystal Green

TAMING THE TEXAS PLAYBOY

CRYSTAL GREEN

Silhouette®

SPECIAL EDITION®

Published by Silhouette Books

America's Publisher of Contemporary Romance

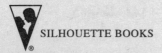

SILHOUETTE BOOKS

ISBN-13: 978-0-373-65585-4

TAMING THE TEXAS PLAYBOY

PLEASE RECYCLE
THIS PRODUCT IS RECYCLABLE

Recycling programs
for this product may
not exist in your area.

Visit Silhouette Books at www.eHarlequin.com

Printed in U.S.A.

Books by Crystal Green

Silhouette Special Edition

His Arch Enemy's Daughter #1455
The Stranger She Married #1498
There Goes the Bride #1522
**Her Montana Millionaire* #1574
The Black Sheep Heir #1587
The Millionaire's Secret Baby #1668
†*A Tycoon in Texas* #1670
††*Past Imperfect* #1724
The Last Cowboy #1752
The Playboy Takes a Wife #1838
~*Her Best Man* #1850
§*Mommy and the Millionaire* #1887
§*The Second-Chance Groom* #1906
§*Falling for the Lone Wolf* #1932
‡*The Texas Billionaire's Bride* #1981
~~*When the Cowboy Said I Do* #2072
§§*Made for a Texas Marriage* #2093
§§*Taming the Texas Playboy* #2103

Silhouette Romance

Her Gypsy Prince #1789

Silhouette Bombshell

The Huntress #28
Baited #112

Harlequin Blaze

Innuendo #261
Jinxed! #303
  "Tall, Dark & Temporary"
The Ultimate Bite #334
One for the Road #387
Good to the Last Bite #426
When the Sun Goes Down #472

*Kane's Crossing
**Montana Mavericks: The Kingsleys
†The Fortunes of Texas: Reunion
††Most Likely To…
~Montana Mavericks: Striking It Rich
§The Suds Club
‡The Foleys and the McCords
~~Montana Mavericks: Thunder Canyon Cowboys
§§Billionaire Cowboys, Inc.

CRYSTAL GREEN

lives near Las Vegas, where she writes for the Silhouette Special Edition and Harlequin Blaze lines. She loves to read, overanalyze movies and TV programs, practice yoga and travel when she can. You can read more about her at www.crystal-green.com, where she has a blog and contests. Also, you can follow her on Facebook at www.facebook.com/people/Chris-Marie-Green/1051327765 and Twitter at www.twitter.com/ChrisMarieGreen.

To Cindy and Dani, who were meant for each other.
And for Mari, who brought them together.

Chapter One

Most people didn't ignore a powerful tycoon like Jeremiah Barron.

But one lady in particular had dared, and here she was, standing by herself in front of the open French windows of a spacious marble lounge in a country mansion near Austin.

The sheer curtains billowed around her in the breeze, her shiny platinum hair rolled back in a chignon, her lithe figure dressed in a cool, white late-summer sheath. Outside, the sound of children's laughter floated from the sunset-lit hedges in the garden maze, and she had a look of such yearning on her face that Jeremiah couldn't take his eyes off of her.

Allison Gale, philanthropist and socialite.

An heiress who'd fallen on misfortune.

The woman Jeremiah hadn't been able to shake from

his mind ever since she'd oh-so-politely put him in his place over a month ago.

As he visually drank her in, his heart fell straight down until it crashed into his gut. But it was only intrigued admiration, really, and it was all Jeremiah was capable of.

Ally—that's what he'd overheard her friends call her—must have sensed that she wasn't by herself anymore, and as she glanced at him, she didn't have quite enough time to erase the longing from her expression.

As if she'd been exposed in some way, Ally abandoned the window, folding her hands in front of her, the epitome of the elegant cohostess for the annual Help for Children fund-raising weekend.

"I didn't hear you come in, Mr. Barron," she said, smiling. "Welcome to the Howard ranch."

"So formal," he said as he dropped the hand holding his Stetson over his heart to his side. "I've asked you before to use my given name. And I'd think that a visit to the country would call for some casualness."

As she strolled away from the window, the children kept laughing outside, and she held on to a wisp of a smile before she gestured toward the sounds.

"Dinner's still being served on the patio," she said. "The Howards' kids are having ice cream for dessert, but we can still bring you something more substantial."

"I'm solid as can be."

She walked right by him, making no comment, leaving a trail of cherry-blossom scent that made his head light, his belly clench.

Maybe she was remembering the Red Cross event about a month ago, when he'd seen her in the crowd.

He'd been drawn by her classic blond beauty, making his way over to her, grinning at her, just as he did whenever he wanted to talk someone into something.

Rumor had it that Ally Gale's bank account had taken a hit lately, and although you couldn't tell from her polished style, Jeremiah had wondered if she missed fine wine and dining. If she'd want a man who could promise some of that to her.

She'd stopped him before he'd gotten much further.

Mr. Barron, she'd said with a note of amusement, along with a tone that told him she was well aware of his reputation. *I think you've got a roomful of women who're just waiting for you to ask* them *for a dance.*

And she'd left him standing there, as stranded as a castaway on a deserted island.

But what Ally Gale hadn't known was that she'd presented a challenge to a man who thrived on them, both as copresident of his family's corporation and in a personal life that had allowed him to forget more and more lately about the Barron Group.

Especially since the scandal had hit a few months ago.

"I'm surprised you even came—and so early, before everyone else," she said as he sauntered behind her out of the lounge and into the foyer, where a grand, curved staircase waited.

They stopped at the foot of it, Jeremiah lingering near her. She drew in a short breath, but otherwise she kept that polite smile on her face.

"I didn't see any reason for waiting to come here," he said, his voice low.

Ally seemed to realize that he was talking about more

than just attending a charity function, and she took a step away.

"Well, we appreciate your donation and participation this weekend. I'll check to see that the butler has taken your bags to your room."

Was she already dismissing him?

His hackles rose. He'd been dismissed by his father all his life, and that was what had taught him to fight. The instinct was too ingrained for him to ignore it now.

Still, his tone was nonchalant.

"Signing up for a long weekend here in the country is just what the doctor ordered. A lungful of fresh air to be gotten while contributing to a good cause."

"So says the corporate mogul," she said. "I know you're also here to wheel and deal with a few other businessmen, too. It's the perfect opportunity, with so many of you staying on the premises."

Okay, so the event was driven by donors who'd paid to reside in the luxurious French-style country house on a massive ranch for an extended weekend of Texas barbecuing, an auction and a fancy cowboy ball. There *would* be a lot of opportunity at hand. In particular, Jeremiah had been sweet-talking the cohosts and owners of this ranch, the Howards, because they had a few properties that had caught his eye as a developer.

But Ally was the real organizer of this party—and when he'd found out that she was the cohostess, it had been icing on the cake.

It stung Jeremiah's pride that she was subtly dancing around any flirtation, but it also pushed him on. Better to be engaged in a chase like this than to think about what was going on back home at his family's ranch. Better to lose himself in the arms of another woman who could make him forget—a woman like Ally. If she would just give in to him now, rather than later.

"All right, business is on the agenda," he said. "As a matter of fact, *you* still hold a property that I'd like to chat about—your abandoned hotel near Galveston. It's got a prime location, and it'd be just right for another one of our golf resorts."

"No business for me this weekend, thank you."

Jeremiah walked toward her, his boot steps heavy on the marble floor, echoing off the tall, crown-molded ceilings.

Her eyes widened—blue-green eyes that would put most seas to shame.

Jeremiah's belly swirled with need, just at thinking of what it would feel like to undo her light hair, feel it tumble out of that fancy chignon and over his hands as he brushed his fingertips against the back of her neck….

Before the fantasy could continue, she pulled him out of it.

"I wish your family could've attended, too. It's a shame. I know your father enjoyed it last year when he came."

Awkwardness slammed into the room, and judging by her expression, Ally seemed to realize she'd strayed into dangerous territory.

"My dad's resting," he said, because it sounded much better than the truth—that Eli Barron was reeling from what he'd done to his family, drinking too much. Hell, when he'd announced to the public that he'd fathered a son, Chet, with his sister-in-law, there'd been a huge scandal. It had been contained by a PR firm, of course, though the fallout had rocked all the Barrons, especially after the recent death of Uncle Abe, the cuckolded husband.

Jeremiah glanced away, steeling himself against the pain of his uncle's passing, plus the entire scandal itself. But when he looked back at Ally, one glimpse of this woman, with such pale skin, pink lips and mermaid eyes, sent him to a place where none of his problems existed.

The distractions always worked. At least for a time.

Putting this particular discussion behind them, he took a chance, rising from his carefree stance against the stair rail to be nearer to Ally. Her dress was sleeveless, so he could just about sense the warmth from her bare arms. He could smell her cherry-blossom scent again, too.

Cherries and heat, he thought. Moonlight and blond hair fanned over the sheets of his bed….

His voice was low. "My family's fine now, Ally. We've moved on."

She raised her face in order to meet his gaze. He could tell that she wanted to snap their visual connection, back away from him, but she wasn't doing it.

A brutal thrill sawed at his chest, then traveled lower, ripping and opening a hole that needed to be filled.

With her.

With…

There was another need that he couldn't identify, but it didn't matter now. She was the one who'd politely rejected him, sparking a feeling in him that he couldn't seem to access anymore. And when she eventually changed her mind about him, she would get him through that night and on to the next, where he would find someone else to pull him out of this "descent," or whatever his brother Tyler kept calling it.

Leave it to Ty, the golden boy, to know better.

Slowly, so as not to break the moment, Jeremiah brushed Ally's arm with his fingertips. Goosebumps came in the wake of his touch.

He *did* do something to her, and she couldn't deny it.

But she tried, and he didn't expect anything less.

"I should really check on your room," she said, circumventing him and taking the stairs.

This time, Jeremiah didn't follow her.

Like every deal he embarked upon, Ally Gale would close, and it was only a matter of time before she realized it.

Thank goodness there would be no other guests arriving until tomorrow morning, long before the big barbecue, because Ally was in no state to greet them now.

She stood in front of the air conditioner in the guest room she'd been assigned for the weekend, hoping it would cool her off.

No such luck.

Darn it—she was acting like a silly teenager with a crush, just because Jeremiah Barron had whisked his fingers over her arm. What was next—an entire meltdown if he should happen to put his hand on the small of her back during a dance at the ball?

But, even as she chided herself, the memory of that brush against her arm torched away at her, starting in her tummy then trickling outward in wiggles of heat that settled low and deep within her.

Wonderful.

She blew out a breath. Maybe she was just lonely. It had been that way ever since she and Marco Terelli had gone their separate ways early this year. He was an international businessman who constantly traveled, but she'd been optimistic about their chances. She'd even thought that he actually had intentions, plans with her, but the longer he'd put them off, the more certain she'd become that he was in their relationship for nothing more than occasional companionship.

Heck, though—she'd done fine on her own ever since the breakup. There'd been a few dates for her, yet nothing that had really stoked her interest.

At least not until Jeremiah Barron had shown up at that Red Cross event, a cowboy magnate with a subtle swagger. Every woman on the lawn of the cocktail party had been watching him—including Ally, although it had just been a few seconds before she'd turned away from the notorious playboy.

She had too much dignity for one-night stands, and that probably was all Jeremiah Barron would offer. That was what she'd told herself, anyway.

Then he'd approached *her,* and it had been like a jolt to her system, a twist to her straight-arrow nature. She'd gently nipped in the bud any ideas he might've had about her, of course, and she'd thought that would be that.

Why would he want her, anyway? She wasn't his usual flash-and-dash type of woman. Everyone knew that Allison Gale actually was rather quiet, a homebody, even before her financial situation had changed, making her cut back on everything from the money she often donated to her favorite causes to vacations that she'd decided she didn't really need after all.

But, just minutes ago, when she'd been alone with Jeremiah Barron, she'd felt the same adrenalized rush from that night. Then, today, she'd made that blunder—bringing up his family scandal—and, in spite of herself, she'd tried to make up for it, but only because it was in her nature to comfort people.

It was just that when she'd seen him looking so sad, his eyes a faraway blue, it had tugged at her. Jeremiah Barron, the whip-smart billionaire of the Barron Group—a man who was so in control that he had his pick of any woman he wanted, in Texas and beyond—had been just as vulnerable as any other person at that moment.

But then he'd seemed to realize that he was revealing too much, and the playboy in him had returned.

Ally turned her back to the air conditioner, allowing the coolness to bathe the back of her neck. There was good reason she couldn't give in to a temptation like him. A *very* good one.

Her gaze strayed to the mahogany Chippendale nightstand near her spacious, white-coverlet-draped bed. On top of the table, next to an old-fashioned Tiffany lamp, a portfolio of copied pages waited. Ally had been going through it every night, praying, hoping…

A knock brought her away from the air conditioner and to the side of the bed, where she'd slipped off her strappy high-heeled sandals. She slid them back on just before she opened the door.

At the sight of Aunt Jess, with her tanned skin, sun-streaked brunette hair and purple-wildflower wrap-around dress, Ally gave a little cry and hugged her.

"You weren't supposed to be here until tomorrow!" Ally said.

"I caught an earlier flight."

Jess squeezed her until Ally thought she would die of lost breath. Then her aunt, who'd just turned forty this year and didn't look a bit of it, held Ally away from her.

"Aren't you something to behold," Jess said, just before she hugged Ally one last time and stepped inside the room. She was carrying a brightly woven straw bag, and she spilled the contents onto the bed. "I was thinking of you while I was in Maui."

Ally picked up one of ten boxes of chocolate-covered macadamia nuts. "Aunt Jess, you're out to make me gain weight."

"You could eat fifty boxes and never put on an ounce. You make me sick."

"But you thought you'd see if this tactic worked anyway?" Ally began to undo the plastic wrapping. "Let's put that theory to the test."

Jess laughed and pinched Ally's cheek, just as if her niece was still a toddler. Jess was only a decade older, but she'd always wielded those years over Ally.

Then, after roaming to the other side of the bed, she plopped down onto the mattress. "I can't wait for the barbecue tomorrow. Texas beef. I missed it while I was away."

"There'll be plenty of it."

"There's always plenty of everything when you're in charge."

Ally bit into a candy, rolling her eyes with pleasure. She offered the box to Jess, who refused it. Ally noticed that her blue eyes were shining with emotion.

"I know I've been telling you this for a while now," Jess said, "but if your parents were around to see how you've taken up their causes…"

Ally's smile won out over the sadness. The anguish of losing her parents in a small plane crash—they'd been traveling to yet another philanthropic event—had diminished, but not disappeared. It never would, even though they'd died just over a year ago.

"At least," Jess continued, "they didn't live to see what happened to their holdings. Your dad just should've forced *you* to take over the company."

"Or you." Most of the Gale Company's media properties had been driven to bankruptcy by the cousins and protégés her father had trusted, their fortunes weakened by Ponzi schemes and other bad investments. Ally had told her parents early on that she preferred not to run the business and would rather carry on with their charity work, and they had made provisions for her and Jess to do so.

Sometimes she wished she'd made a different choice, though, even if she wasn't a businessperson at heart. At least she had managed her own, more modest personal accounts decently; though she wasn't stinking rich anymore, she wasn't broke. She even had a couple of business properties left, including that Galveston resort Jeremiah Barron had talked about.

And she really should think about selling it to him.

But what would happen if she conducted business with an attractive rake who was clearly intent on doing more than paperwork?

She chased off the possibility. She was concerned about her finances, but she wouldn't put herself into a situation where she was figuratively in bed with Jeremiah Barron.

Not since she'd realized what *really* mattered in life after she'd broken things off with Marco.

Jess had noticed the portfolio on Ally's nightstand and gone for it, opening it up before Ally could say anything.

"What's this?" she asked.

Ally sat next to her on the bed. "I've been meaning to tell you something."

Nerves skittered through her as her aunt held up the folder, perusing a copy of a collage Ally had put together—a mosaic of photos that revealed what she loved in life: rainbows she had seen on walks through the countryside when she'd been growing up on her parents' Texas estate ranch, which had recently been sold off. Her favorite horse, an Arabian named Willow, who had died a couple of years ago. The lights of San Antonio's Riverwalk at night through the window of the luxury apartment that she'd recently said goodbye to. A picture of the relatively humble country house she'd bought in central California over a year ago and managed to hold on to, with its few rolling green acres, oak trees, big windows and tiny personal vineyard.

"You had time to do an art project lately, Al?" Jess asked, laying the portfolio on the mattress.

Ally swallowed. She hadn't told anyone about the reason for that portfolio yet. Then again, she didn't have any other close family besides Aunt Jess, and her younger friends in this social set wouldn't understand.

"I'm going to have a child, Jess."

Her aunt looked as if she'd been zapped with a stun gun.

"What I mean," Ally said, "is that I'm planning to adopt."

Another zap for Jess, who still remained uncharacteristically speechless.

Ally rushed to finish. "I've thought about this a long time. It even started back with Marco, after I realized that we didn't love each other enough to get married and begin a family. He loved his business pursuits, and he was never around, which wasn't the kind of life I wanted for me or any children. So, shortly after we broke up, I applied to an independent adoption facilitator in California." She motioned toward the portfolio. "They wanted me to do this so the birth moms could get an idea of who I am before any of them request an interview. I just turned it in about a month and a half ago—"

"Wow."

Ally startled at her aunt's wary tone.

But then she went on.

"I'm not willing to wait around for Mr. Right. I'm ready for children *now*. I might not be rich any longer, but I'm still pretty well-off, and I can afford to give a family a really good life." She took the portfolio from the bed. "Besides, I want to do what Mom and Dad did for me."

She'd been adopted, too, and although the process had been a closed one, her parents had told her the truth early on, emphasizing that Ally was all theirs, no matter the circumstances of her birth.

Jess shifted on the bed. "You're doing this all on your own?"

"Yes."

"And you've thought about every detail?"

"Of course."

But Jess still seemed uncomfortable, and Ally knew the exact reason—she'd been afraid it would play a part in Jess's opinion.

"Don't you think," her aunt said, "you should wait a little longer? You know how I felt about my mom raising me by herself—she wasn't equipped for it after my dad left. Even with the nannies and our money, there was still a lack of…" Jess sighed. "Ally, I *needed* a father there. I know that you're capable of being a wonderful mother, but half of the equation is still going to be missing for that child."

"I don't agree with that, Jess."

She didn't have the heart to tell her aunt that just because a man was around, it didn't guarantee a happy home life. She'd seen too many marriages with children falter and break in their high-society world.

Jess blew out a breath. "You lost your parents not too long ago, then came Marco. I'm afraid you're basing your choice on the wrong feelings."

"I'm not rebounding or being rash."

"I just…" Jess wrinkled her brow. "You've got a lot of time to be a mother, Al."

Ally slowly stood from the bed, clutching the portfolio.

"You, of all people, should know that I wouldn't take this lightly. I'm not some flippant socialite with a whim."

And that was why she was steering a hundred feet clear of men like Jeremiah Barron—at least on an intimate basis. It was well and fine to associate with them during the charity events, but her parents had raised her to see through money and all its trappings—and Jeremiah was the peak of its excesses.

She put him out of her head—and everywhere else—as she went to the closet, where she'd stored her suitcase, and put the portfolio on top of the luggage.

"Ally…" Jess said, pressing a hand to her temple.

Why couldn't her aunt understand?

"I want to be there for someone," Ally said, "just like Mom and Dad. They gave me such love, Jess, more than my birth parents could've ever done." Since her adoption had been a closed one, she hadn't been able to contact the woman who'd given birth to her, much less the man who'd fathered her. Ally used to dream that she would meet them someday, but they'd obviously never wanted to find her.

Ally wasn't going to do that to her child, though; this would be an open adoption, and she would see to it that her child never wondered, creating impossible fantasies about the people who had given her or him up.

"They raised me right," Ally added, "and they gave me values as well as making *me* valued. And I can pay that forward."

"Without a father around?"

"I'm not ruling out that there might be someone who can be the baby's father someday," Ally said. "But that could take years, and I'm not willing to wait, not when I have so much to give now."

"So there's no way you'll take more time before some birth mother takes a liking to you."

Ally closed the closet door. She could understand why her aunt was thinking that the hurt Marco had visited upon her was translating into a need for a child, and that Ally was rushing into something because she only wanted some validation.

Was she only thinking of herself, believing that she would be enough family for a child?

No, Ally thought. That wasn't true at all.

And she wanted to convince Jess of it.

The next morning, before breakfast was served in the dining room, Ally got ready early, showering and putting on some jeans and a pale blue blouse that tied at her waist. Then she set out for a stroll before the heat really claimed the weather.

She and Jess hadn't talked anymore last night about the adoption. But even as her aunt had changed the subject and chatted about Hawaii until they retired, Ally knew that she would find a way to change Jess's mind about raising a child without a father. She yearned for her aunt's unconditional support, and she wanted to make darned sure it came sooner rather than later.

While walking the meadows, Ally felt the sun on her skin as it rose, the warmth breathing over her arms. Grass swayed in the slight breeze and, in the distance, horses wandered in a pasture.

She bent to pick a purple wildflower, wondering what a baby's face would look like the first time he or she saw one. Wondering how it would feel to hold a newborn as day turned to night and she rocked her child to sleep.

Lost in the beauty of that thought, she didn't hear the grumble of a Jeep until she glanced up to find it beside her on the road.

And the second she saw the driver, dressed in faded jeans, a white Western shirt and a cowboy hat, her pulse twirled in her veins.

Jeremiah Barron.

He swept off his hat. "Mornin', Ally."

His wheat-colored hair looked tousled and he had that devil-may-care glint in those blue eyes, which always seemed to be in a near squint, as if he was forever about to crack a charming grin.

Then he unleashed a full smile on Ally, putting his hat back on his head. Her chest flared with that unwelcome response he always brought out in her—the "no-no-uh-uh" explosion of tingly awareness.

But he wasn't what she needed in her life right now. Just imagine the trouble a scallywag like him would bring to a new mother who didn't need it.

"Early riser?" she asked, striving to be sociable.

"I figured I'd take a look around, check out the sights."

There went that glimmer in his eyes again, and Ally couldn't put a halt to the flutter in her chest.

But she tried. "Have fun then, Mr. Barron."

"Jeremiah," he said lightly. "We already talked about the first-name thing, Ally."

She should tell him once and for all that she was more comfortable using the "mister," but then she recalled yesterday when he'd looked so melancholy after she'd brought up his family.

He was a person, not just a mister, and she didn't have the heart to treat him like something less.

That was as far as it would go, though.

"How was your room?" she asked. "Terrence took care of you?"

"Terrence is all a butler should be."

As the motor purred, Jeremiah eyed her, and it unsettled her that she most definitely knew he had something other than butlers in mind.

"Okay, then." She nodded at him, thinking that it would be a good idea to continue with her walk.

But as soon as she strolled ahead, there was a stir behind her, as if he'd gotten out of the vehicle and—

Jeremiah's arm wrapped around Ally's waist just before he scooped her up and deposited her in the passenger seat.

What the…?

Breath knocked out of her, Ally clung to the seat as Jeremiah jogged to the other side, hopped in and revved the engine to a go.

"Just turning your morning walk into a morning adventure," he said with a sexy grin.

As they took off, Ally held tight, knowing that with Jeremiah Barron, this was bound to be more than a morning jaunt.

It would be a wild ride that she couldn't afford.

Chapter Two

Jeremiah didn't give Ally a chance to protest as he drove along.

He let it ride, enjoying himself, trying not to think about how, this morning, he'd called home to check up on his dad—how hungover the old man might be today.

And it had been just as Jeremiah had expected— Eli Barron was *very* hungover and the household was walking around on eggshells. To add to that, Jeremiah's cousin…no, *brother*…Chet had left the ranch again, taking off to oversee another business deal somewhere, just as confused about his new family situation as anyone else.

With all that pressing down on Jeremiah, he'd been dying to let off steam, especially since he'd also endured a night of thinking about how Ally Gale was somewhere in that mansion, down a hall, just a short walk away.

Then he'd seen her strolling in the meadow and, suddenly, the morning had gotten a little brighter.

"*Jeremiah,*" Ally said, leaning away from him as they drove down the road, "I want to walk, not..."

He slowed down. "Not what?"

He'd said it with an innuendo in his tone, and he noticed that there were goosebumps on Ally's arms again.

Instead of answering his question, she rolled her eyes.

As they traveled toward some cottonwoods, Jeremiah caught the scent of Ally's hair, which she'd tucked up into that chignon again. It smelled so good, like summer fruit. Same with her skin. And he couldn't stop looking at the graceful curve of her neck and wondering what she would do if he just stopped the Jeep, leaned over and sketched his lips over her....

"You just can't do these kinds of things," she said.

"You mean sweeping you away for a ride kinds of things?"

Another sigh. "Yes."

"Ah." He slowed down even more as they entered the copse of trees, on a rougher road that was marked by tire tracks. Next to them, a creek burbled over rocks and moss. Up ahead, a rabbit darted into a bush. "Dangerous stuff, isn't it? Riding in a vehicle with me."

"You know exactly what I mean."

"What's so wicked about it?"

"You have more than a morning ride in mind," she said. "We both know that."

"Ally." His voice was gritty. "I'm not that bad of a guy."

She only laughed and, for some reason, it nicked him.

What—did he want acceptance from the socialite who was so well-known for her upstanding morals?

Not *acceptance,* really. But even if he did, why should he care what she thought of him beyond how good he could make them both feel?

"You think I'm out to ruin your reputation," he said.

"Not necessarily. But I really don't need the kind of gossip that's bound to happen if someone sees me alone in the woods with you."

"You're above gossip."

"No one is."

She was a tough one under all the polish. No wonder Allison Gale had never fallen prey to trappings of the high life—drugs, decadence, the loss of a moral center—as most of their circle had. She'd risen above the temptations, so why shouldn't she be able to withstand him, too?

It weighed Jeremiah down to be classified along with those other bad influences.

"Speaking of gossip," Ally said, "*you* should know more than anyone how destructive it can be."

"I don't let it bother me."

This time, she did look at him, and the vivid hue and honesty of her blue-green eyes rattled him.

"I think the scandal bothers you a lot," she said softly. "Even though you give good interviews to the press on behalf of the Barron Group, and even though you seem to stand strong for your family's businesses with the storm brewing around you, it all matters in some way to you. You just don't like to show it."

He let her go on thinking so.

"You know there's been idle talk about you," she added. "Some downright mean comments."

"I haven't noticed."

But her words ate at him. No one outside the family knew him well enough to be talking. They didn't know how his family had always operated: Tyler, the golden son, raised and bred to be the leader of the family, then Jeremiah, the afterthought, who watched from the shadows. Their father had never expected much out of him, but it wasn't in Jeremiah's Barron blood to fade to irrelevance, although he often felt that disposable.

No, he had quietly gone about becoming his own man while growing up, working his own deals, whether it was talking his way into better grades at prep school and college, making rogue deals for the good of the Barron Group early on in his career or independently negotiating for the best horse stock in Texas to fill the stables at the family's estate ranch.

Unlike his brother, who'd gotten divorced, and his father, who'd failed with his own wife, Jeremiah had taken another route altogether. He'd stayed on his own, playing the field. He'd always been good at it, too. And, perversely, even though he and Tyler had never been at odds, Jeremiah took some satisfaction that, at least in this area, he was the better brother, always succeeding with the women, never letting one down.

And he was better than his father at that game, too, which mattered more. So much more.

Then Chet had come along, and Tyler had wrestled with his own issues at being replaced as the favorite son in the family, since their dad had gone overboard in making sure their "new" brother felt loved. It'd taken Zoe Velez, the PR woman tasked with cleaning up Eli's mess, to save Tyler. And it was good to see that she made him happy, and that he made her feel the same way.

But Jeremiah hadn't needed anyone to save him. He'd only distanced himself from the family, preferring the nightlife. Preferring to succeed where his father still hadn't—in having no strings attached to his pleasures, in finding happiness *that* way.

Value. For a few hours, he could matter to someone, and that very idea was what kept him going.

Ally had apparently been waiting for a more dramatic response from him, but when he didn't provide it, she said, "You don't care about what people are saying?"

"Why should I?"

"I would care." She paused. "Some say that you take after your dad in the lothario department."

Jeremiah withstood the blow. "There's a big difference between me and my father."

"And what's that?"

He laughed, low and tight. "I've never had anything to do with married women…especially a sister-in-law. I'd *never* do that to Tyler." He hesitated. "Or to Chet."

She tilted her head, and Jeremiah found himself talking when he shouldn't have been.

"I guess I'm still getting used to the fact that Chet and I are brothers, not cousins."

"I hear he's having a hard time, too."

Jeremiah shrugged, but he knew that in reality Chet was spinning out of control in his own way, losing himself in work, just as surely as Jeremiah did sometimes when that free-falling sensation grabbed onto him—a feeling that he was separate from everything, everyone.

Irrelevant, even.

But when Ally kept looking at him—not away from him—he actually found something to latch onto.

Long eyelashes, deep blue-green eyes that he could float in…

"I believe you," she said. "You wouldn't hurt anyone like that. You're not that kind of man."

Then she faced forward again.

Jeremiah wasn't sure he'd heard her correctly. Had she just said something nice about him?

Well, I'll be.

"I'm not sure my dad got together with my aunt Laura because he intended to hurt others," he said. "They were idiots, that's all. They weren't thinking in the least, just…feeling."

His last words seemed to hover, like a faint chill under the shade of the trees.

"We all feel," she said.

It was as if he'd been encased in a box, the lid slamming shut, keeping the most vulnerable areas of himself packed away.

He'd "felt" once, with a woman who reminded him of Ally in a way—sweet, steady and much too good for the likes of him.

He brought the Jeep to a stop, put it in neutral with the parking brake on, and she stiffened in her seat, as if expecting trouble from him.

"Don't worry," he said. "I'm not about to make a pass."

"I didn't expect one."

Right. She still had those goosebumps on her arms.

"You seem a little skittish around me, Ally. Or are you just that way in general?"

"I'm not skittish about anything." Her spine seemed to gain even more steel.

What would it take to melt her? Everyone had a finessing point, a button to push, an abracadabra moment that opened her up. As an heiress who'd lost so much lately, could Ally be swayed by what she couldn't afford anymore?

Diamonds? Trips to Europe?

Jeremiah wasn't sure, because she was tougher to read than most.

But, while he was here in the country, he might as well find her abracadabra.

"What if," he said, "after this weekend is over, we had dinner together?"

"Why?"

Not the answer he'd been hoping for. "Why not?"

"You don't do casual dinners."

He laughed. "You think I go into everything with an agenda, is that it?"

"They don't call you a shark for nothing."

Zing. She got him.

"I was just thinking of taking you somewhere nice, like Chez Gisele in Dallas," he said. "We could discuss that Galveston property. Or," he said, grinning, "we could have a hell of a business discussion here."

Ally still looked straight ahead. "I see where you're going with this, and it's not just about any business deal."

Jeremiah leaned back in his seat, surrendering. For now.

She seemed to notice, relaxing slightly until she saw the expression he was wearing, no doubt one of consideration.

"What now?" she asked.

"Just wondering. What did Marco Terelli have that other men don't? How did *he* get into your good graces?"

At the mention of her ex-boyfriend, Ally seemed to withdraw into herself.

"It wasn't what he had," she said. "It's what I thought he wanted. But we found out that we were on different timetables."

What she thought he wanted?

Jeremiah recalled last evening, when he'd witnessed Ally staring out the window of the lounge, seeming so wistful as she watched the children outside.

All his inner playboy alarms rang simultaneously.

But as a slight breeze floated her scent to Jeremiah, the heat combed through him again, taking him over. He wanted to reach out, grasp a stray lock of her hair between his fingers, test the silk of it, imagine how it would feel against his bare chest as she nuzzled him.

She unbuckled her safety belt, obviously intending to ditch him.

"I think it's time for me to start walking again," she said.

This time, she was deadly serious about being let out of the car.

"Yes, ma'am," he said.

He tried not to let the heaviness in his chest get him

down as he automatically exited the Jeep and went around to the other side to offer a hand as she stepped down.

But just as soon as he assumed the role of a gentleman, she slipped to the driver's seat.

"Maybe you need some cooling off," she said, indicating the creek. "The water should be bracing this time of the morning."

And, with that, she started up the vehicle and drove away.

As she disappeared at a curve on the road, behind some trees, Jeremiah pushed back his cowboy hat.

Okay then. She hadn't dismissed him outright. As a matter of fact, she'd given him tit for tat. Maybe she'd even been…

Flirting?

Doubtful. She'd taken some pains to point out the differences between them and they stuck to Jeremiah like a stain now that he had nothing here but the quiet chirp of birds and the gurgle of the creek.

He started to walk out of the woods, feeling as if he was back in the shadows, unable to leave the darkness behind.

After Ally returned the Jeep to the garages, explaining that Jeremiah Barron had decided to take a walk by the creek and had handed his ride off to her, she started her day in earnest.

Thank goodness she had a lot of hostessing to do. Otherwise, she wouldn't have been able to accomplish anything but think about their encounter. Even hours later, after she'd greeted the arriving guests who would be staying in the rooms and then made sure they were settled, her skin was still alive with the memory of Jeremiah sitting in the seat next to her.

As she thought of what he might've had in mind when he'd scooped her into the Jeep and taken her off to the private woods, her blood fizzed.

What if she'd just relaxed and allowed herself to scoot closer to him?

Now as she came down the grand staircase, her belly flip-flopped and she hoped no one would notice her high color once she got outside, where the Texas-style barbecue was already in progress.

Forget Jeremiah Barron, she told herself. He had no place in what she wanted out of life.

Just inside the door, she smoothed down the red-and-white gingham blouse she was wearing with her blue jeans and boots. She'd woven her hair into a low braid, and she wasn't exactly the elegant socialite right now. Maybe she'd even played down her looks so that Jeremiah would take a second glance at her and completely lose interest. Besides, this was how she'd look from now on—a woman who'd been taken down a peg or two, but one who was going to be a lot happier, even without all the money.

When she opened the door, the expansive lawn greeted her with its rush of kids running around, its tent pavilions decorating the green. She didn't see Jeremiah at first and, relieved, she went toward the barbecuing area, where the aromas of hickory and beef wafted in the air.

Aunt Jess had put herself in charge of the caterers, so Ally left her to it, then checked inside the main tent, where an adults-only cocktail gathering was going strong. Donors—both those who had paid an exorbitant amount to stay in rooms on the Howards' property and those who had just come in for tonight's event—greeted her in their cowboy getups.

When Rich and Stef Howard, the owners of the property, saw Ally from across the tent, they waved, and she went to them.

Stef, a dark-haired, doe-eyed beauty, showed off her belt buckle, with its solid silver coils curving in sinuous patterns. The Howards could very well afford items like this with the money they made from oil.

"See what I'm auctioning off later tonight?" she asked.

Her husband, a tall, tanned man in his new jeans and short-sleeved checkered shirt, hugged his wife to him. "Stef had it custom-made after she designed it."

"It's amazing," Ally said.

"And it should fetch a pretty price," Rich said. "Hopefully the rest of the auction, plus the plate charge and the room rentals, will do the rest." The Help for Children Foundation, which reached out to homeless kids, was their pet cause. "We don't know how to thank you for all your hard work, Ally."

If only they realized how hard she'd worked to make up for what she could've once given in cash to the charity.

Stef said, "Your parents would be so proud of you."

Ally smiled, squeezed Stef's arm, then made her way to the auction tent, where the auctioneer was warming up. Afterward, it was off to the barbecue area with all its rented picnic tables, and then to the open field where the kids' games had been set up.

Children—from the sons and daughters of donors to the ones that the foundation aided—were everywhere. They laughed while riding the ponies, jumped up and down at the game booths, which featured carnival-type balloon games and ring tosses that gave out stuffed animals as prizes. They ran in foot races and gunnysack races.

Emotion closed Ally's throat as she watched it all.

Their gaiety made even a residence that wasn't hers into a home, and as Ally saw a little girl with blond curls running by, her heart just about broke with wanting.

No matter what Aunt Jess said, Ally knew she was going to have a happy family of her own. Even if she had to raise a child all by herself—if she was lucky enough to be chosen by a birth mother—then she would've found something to complete her existence. She wasn't naive enough to believe that raising a child would be all lollipops and laughs, but she was ready for even the hard times. It would be worth every tribulation and smile.

She watched the little blonde girl arrive at a fortress of hay bales, where kids were lassoing straw horses and—

Ally's pulse burst when she saw the last person she expected to be enjoying himself around kids circling a lasso over his head and then effortlessly snagging a straw horse before hauling it in.

Jeremiah.

Shouldn't he be in the cocktail tent?

But, no, there he was, bending down to the newly arrived blond-curled moppet, tipping back his hat and showing her how to hold a rope. Then, when he picked the girl up and helped her to lasso a straw horse, he cheered with the child, whose face glowed as if she had succeeded in the task all by herself.

Ally warmed and, when Jeremiah turned around and saw her, the warmth turned into a conflagration, piercing her, making her ache.

Their gazes locked, as if something had clicked and, for once, he didn't have a rake's lowered tilt to his expression.

He seemed…happy.

Just plain happy.

But then, just as Ally was starting to look at Jeremiah Barron in a different light, something snapped.

A moment of realization in him?

But why? What was so bad about Ally seeing him like this?

He put the little girl back down, leaving her with the rope, as he turned around and walked toward the cocktail tent.

Jeremiah's mind was stretching apart, as if it didn't know which way to go.

Why should it bother him that Ally had seen him goofing around with the kids? Didn't Tyler often tell him that he was nothing more than an overgrown child himself?

Maybe it was in the way that Ally had been watching him, with such expectation. She probably thought that she'd caught him in an unguarded situation, that he'd revealed something about himself that no one really ever recognized about him.

But she was wrong. All Jeremiah had done was make a detour over to that lasso station, thinking it might be fun to show the critters a thing or two about roping. It didn't mean he was good at babysitting or relating to anyone beyond his social set.

It didn't mean he was going to suddenly get married and have a bunch of rug rats and live happily ever after, either, as his father had so triumphantly proved could never happen with men like them.

Jeremiah entered the cocktail tent, hoping that Ally wouldn't follow. Then he ordered a stiff whiskey.

It didn't take long for him to get back into his comfort zone, thank God, especially when a long-legged oil-field heiress in jeans, with big hair under her Shady Brady, cornered him near the bar.

"Fancy seeing you here," said Bonnie Taylor.

She ran a gaze over his boots, jeans and long-sleeved Western shirt as if she'd never seen him garbed like this before. But she probably hadn't. Jeremiah usually attended designer-suit functions.

However, *he* knew Bonnie well, in more than one way. Even so, tonight her curves and brandy-rich voice didn't do it for him.

Jeremiah downed his whiskey and gestured to the bartender for another.

"Ooo," she said. "It's been one of those days, has it?"

"That and more."

"What's bothering my boy?"

Her possessive pillow talk didn't sit well with him, and he realized that, for the first time in his life, he wasn't in the mood for a sure thing.

Bonnie got the drift. Unfortunately, she wasn't the type to take rejection lying down.

"You already have someone scribbled on your dance card tonight?" Then she laughed. "Of course you do. Why did I even ask? Like father, like son."

Jeremiah clutched his glass. For a second, he almost gave into her taunting, itching to pull her to him and show her…show *everyone*…that even if he was like his dad in some ways, he was better at the games they played.

Then Bonnie cleared her throat, and he glanced up to see her eyeing the tent's entrance.

Ally had come in and, damn him, he must've had a blazing poker tell on his face, because Bonnie said, "Mystery solved. I saw you approach Miss Pristine at the Red Cross event about a month ago. You're making a play now, aren't you?"

"Good try, but I'm here to pursue some business with the Howards, among others."

"Yeah, well, have fun."

Bonnie meandered away and, before Jeremiah could prepare himself, Ally had bellied up to the bar, too.

Didn't she know enough to just steer clear, especially after this morning?

"I'll have what he's having," she said to the bartender.

"You know this is the hard stuff," Jeremiah said. It was beyond him to ignore her.

"Do you think I'm a puritan?" she asked as the server gave her the beverage. "I drink socially."

"I guess you do."

He prayed she wouldn't say anything about the

kids, but he might as well have hoped for world peace instead.

"You're quite the cowboy," she said. "You had those children eating out of your hand."

"They're impressionable."

"Has anyone ever told you that you get along pretty well with children?"

The note in her voice matched the yearning he'd seen in her yesterday, and it lured him.

Or, maybe it just intrigued him, just as everything else about her did for the time being.

Ally was smiling at him, and damn it all if he didn't go a little weak in the knees.

"I can't believe I'm saying this," she said, "but you might end up making someone a good husband and father someday."

Why did it sound as if she was testing him?

He built his shields back up right quick, especially because the words sounded so familiar: Harvard, back when he'd been young. A twenty-year-old girl named Nancy, with curly black hair, dark eyes, smooth olive skin and a smile almost like Ally's.

You're good deep down, Nancy had once told him. *You don't want people to know it, but I do.*

A few months later, she wasn't saying stuff like that anymore. And Jeremiah had had no choice but to accept that he was what he was—there'd be no changing it, and anyone who tried to do it to him was going to be sorely disappointed.

He could've played along with Ally's assumptions— pretending he was the good man she thought he could be, just to get her to come closer to him again, then even closer until he had her.

But the thought made Jeremiah's stomach turn. It was one thing to enjoy his women, but fully another to set out to break Ally Gale just so she would give in to him.

He tipped his glass to her, adopting that grin of his, feeling much more comfortable now, even as her own smile faded.

"Don't make the mistake of believing you saw something you didn't, Ally." And he downed the whiskey.

Ally faced away from him so that he couldn't witness her own expression, even though he knew exactly what he'd see.

He always knew, and that's why he ordered another drink, just like the playboy he was.

Chapter Three

The only thing that kept Ally's spirits high throughout the rest of the barbecue was the amount of money the auction and event raised for the kids.

But her mind lingered on Jeremiah.

He'd acted as if she'd caught him in some kind of compromising position, but actually, as he'd stood at the bar with the notorious Bonnie Taylor, there'd been no flirtation going on between them at all. The irony was that Ally hadn't walked in on him seducing another woman or anything tawdry like that.

No, Jeremiah had seemed disturbed because Ally had noticed that he'd been having fun with the kids, though why that was a bad thing, Ally couldn't understand.

Could it be that Jeremiah didn't *want* anyone to see that he was a decent guy? Was it easier for him to get through his family's scandal by pretending that nothing and no one got to him?

She'd even said something she had no business bringing up—the comment about his being a good husband and father. She didn't know what she'd been doing, but when he'd shot her down for the very idea, she'd felt wounded just the same.

Silly for thinking, even in a fantastical sense, that the playboy she was attracted to was really a lamb under the skin of a wolf.

Even so, for the rest of the night, Ally pretty much stayed awake in her bed. It didn't help knowing that Jeremiah was in bed, too…maybe even with another woman.

Come morning, she rose early, telling herself she might be able to grab a nap before the grand Texas ball. But she had no trouble staying awake as she supervised the setup of the ballroom, going over instructions with the staff and making sure that the event would run smoothly, from the dinner to the band that would provide the music.

It actually wasn't until dinner that she even had a moment to dwell on Jeremiah again, and that was only because he wasn't in his seat at the long table, which was filled with china, gleaming silverware and calligraphy-scrawled place cards. Twenty millionaire donors were in attendance—the people who had been staying on the property in the charity rooms. There would be far more in attendance tonight for the ball, though.

Next to Ally, Aunt Jess, who was dressed like a siren in a scarlet silk halter gown and matching lipstick, folded her linen napkin over her lap.

"I hear he took a horse from the stables early this morning and just got back a half hour ago," she said amidst the murmurs from the other diners as they sipped the chilled summer squash soup that had just been served.

Ally tore her gaze away from Jeremiah's seat, which was only a few places down and across the table. "What are you talking about, Jess?"

Her aunt rolled her big blue eyes. "Please. You've only been staring at that empty chair for the last ten minutes." She took up a spoonful of the soup. "He'll be here after he cleans up, I imagine."

She would have to shut this down right away. It was bad enough that Aunt Jess had questioned the idea of an adoption, but if she also thought Ally was silly enough to keep company with a scamp… Well, it just seemed to give Jess's caution some credence.

So Ally acted nonchalant about Jeremiah's absence.

That is, until he *did* arrive.

He knew how to make an entrance, too, especially in a black tuxedo. And although he could've passed muster in a James Bond movie, his tousled, wheaten hair belied the cowboy beneath—the roguish gambler who populated every Western movie with his cocky smile and knowing eyes.

It seemed as if no woman in the room could take her eyes off of him, but Ally finally managed. Not that it was easy, because even though she had her gaze on the soup, all she wanted to do was take another peek at him, just so she could feel her heart give an addictive leap, spurring her pulse to electric speed.

From the corner of her eye, she saw him take his chair. She'd seated him between Stef Howard, her cohostess, and a seventy-five-year-old widow, Mrs. Branford. Neither woman seemed to recall that she was married or too dang old to be flapping her eyelashes at a single man.

"Well, look at you," Mrs. Branford said, hormones practically blooming out of her like returning springtime.

Stef Howard just sat there grinning at Jeremiah until her husband cleared his throat across the table. She winked at her hubby and turned to the guest on her other side, striking up a conversation.

Somehow, Ally got through dinner, although she felt Jeremiah watching her during every bit of it. His gaze seemed to press on her skin, her chest, making her breath come short. In fact, it sounded as if she was breathing too loudly, that her scrambling heartbeat could be heard throughout the room.

What was going on with her? Jeremiah Barron was handsome—she would give him that. But otherwise?

He wasn't an option. She had always been well aware of the traps his kind of overindulgent lifestyle could bring, and now wasn't any time to be giving in to that.

And she kept telling herself this through dessert, then her retreat to the ballroom, where she saw to last-minute details and got ready to welcome the guests.

Of course, Jeremiah was the final one inside, turning her nerves upside down as she waited for him to saunter over to her with that twinkle in his eyes.

Like many of the male guests, he took her hand, bowed to her, raised it to his mouth.

Heaven help her, but at the touch of his lips, a million shivers danced up and down every inch of her body.

He raised his gaze, staying bowed over her hand, grinning.

Unable to talk—if she did, she might fumble over each word—she nodded at him, smiling coolly.

When he straightened up he didn't let go of her hand. He even had the gumption to give her a slow look, from her silk pumps and up, over the fall of her coral-colored dress, over her waist, then the bodice that hugged her breasts.

For a forbidden moment, she felt desirable, tempting enough to justify the full-blown blast of desire in his gaze. His obvious lust echoed in her, ricocheting around, leaving a jarring tweak of welcome damage wherever it hit.

Then she realized where they were—in a roomful of people who all seemed to be staring.

And she realized who she was.

Who *he* was.

As Ally removed her hand from his, she wished she hadn't worn a gown that clung to her curves this way. One that didn't bother to hide the modest attributes that creation had seen fit to give her.

"I spent all day taking a horse out, walking the country," he said, "trying to work you off my mind."

The words of a seducer. And if they hadn't sounded so genuine, it would've been easy to walk away.

Ally was saved by the sound of Stef Howard seizing the microphone and welcoming everyone to the ball. Relieved, she turned around to pay attention to their hostess, hopefully giving Jeremiah a clear signal that she wasn't going to play these games with him.

The strategy worked until the band swung into their first song, a rousing two-step.

In Ally's next breath, she felt her hand in Jeremiah's again, his palm on her waist as he swung her into the country dance just as simply as he'd scooped her into that Jeep yesterday morning.

She'd almost forgotten what it felt like to have a man touching her waist, almost forgotten how big and strong those fingers felt, how the imprint of a hand could burn through material and straight through to the skin.

But she'd never felt a burn like this, and it marked her even deeper, traveling like lightning to the center of her.

Before she even realized it, Jeremiah had danced her out the open French doors and to the patio. The stars peeked over the tall maze hedges, and there seemed to be a rumble in the humid air, a trace of sulfur that hinted at a coming rainfall.

She disengaged from Jeremiah. "You just don't give up, do you?"

"If you told me to get lost, I would."

A dare, and she should have laid it all out there to discourage him.

But she couldn't. Something in her—something she'd never tested before—fixed her feet to the tiles. Something curious. A part of her that had always wondered what it might be like to leave behind the good girl, just for a few minutes.

Jeremiah's grin only grew.

"What're you so happy about?" she asked.

"Just thinking."

She hated to ask about what, but there was a fire crackling low in her, and it felt so good.

But what if Aunt Jess or anyone else saw?

Before she could leave, he loosened his tie, giving him an even more roguish air as he peered around them, no doubt noting the emptiness of the patio.

"We never really wrapped up our discussion from yesterday," he said. "You never did tell me what a man can do to impress you."

"I don't dwell much on that," she said. "Besides, if you're trying to butter me up so that you'll get that Galveston property for a sweet deal, don't waste your time. You should talk to my managers."

But she knew from the intense look he was giving her that business might not be the only reason he had danced her out here.

And he proved it when he said, "You should know what you deserve and you should damned well ask for it…in business or otherwise."

A shiver consumed her as he walked closer.

"Has anyone ever understood just what you wanted, Ally? I almost made the mistake of thinking that, maybe, you missed the high life—the champagne, the vacations on exclusive Caribbean islands, fancy limos. But there's more to you than that." Another step toward her. "I'd like to know just what it is that you want."

He was only a couple of heartbeats away now.

It was time to leave. That would be the safest thing to do. But she'd never heard a man talk to her like this before. Not even Marco had understood that although he could give her all the trinkets in the world, all she wanted was simplicity: things like a home, a future… the chance to read bedtime stories to children and tuck them in at night.

Yet no matter what Jeremiah was telling her right now, she couldn't make the mistake of believing that he meant it. He knew how to use words, this man, and she wouldn't mean anything to him in the end but another conquest.

Another diversion in his march of confused days.

That certain something in her—the sleeping bad girl—thought it might be nice to make him less confused. To reach out and take him in, giving him solace. To feed the fire in her until it scorched parts of her that had never been touched.

What if…?

Ally took a deep breath, realizing she'd been holding it. Good Lord, who did she think she was—the only woman in this world who had the power to change Don Juan?

That was a path to disaster, and she knew better. She'd taken pride in being above those games, too, and when she did become a mother, her child would be the better for her fortitude.

He had come to stand so near that his breath stirred the wisps of hair she'd left loose around her face. He smelled so good, like almonds, sweet but with an earthy twist.

"Just think about it, Ally," he whispered.

Then, as the band played on, he went back into the ballroom, leaving her dizzy with all the good-girl-gone-astray possibilities twirling around in her head.

* * *

The ball went on until the early hours of the morning, but Jeremiah found his way to bed before then.

And he found it *alone*.

But that didn't matter, because Ally was one who would take slow, sweet time to persuade, and he was willing to wait…at least for a little longer.

At dawn, he stood in front of his window, seeing the clouds outside, the scatter of rain. Last night, after he'd left Ally on the patio, he'd stayed at the ball for a time, visiting with the Howards and other business associates, even setting up the promise of a real estate deal or two. All the while, he'd watched Ally tending to her guests.

Had he gotten all those crazy ideas she'd seemed to be entertaining about him out of her head? Those notions about how he might make a decent husband or father one day?

Had he gotten her back to thinking about having an uncomplicated good time instead?

Maybe so, because he'd seen a change in her eyes when he'd told her that he wished he knew what she wanted. He'd seen a craving that hadn't been there before, and it wasn't the same yearning he'd noticed when she'd been watching the kids that day. It burned hotter than that.

He'd reset the stage for a simple wooing of Ally again, all right. Now, he would give her some time to think about what he'd said, checking back with her tonight.

As Jeremiah lathered his face with shaving cream, he thought about how tonight was his last chance; after all, the charity function had come to its conclusion, and he knew she would be departing the ranch tomorrow morning, long after all her guests had gone.

He took a razor to the stubble, but there was something dragging him down from the stimulation of seducing Ally Gale.

Getting to the good girl. It should've sounded so appealing, yet it somehow seemed…tainted.

Yeah, that was the perfect word for it. Ally wasn't like the others who'd fallen to his attentions. Even in the afterglows, he'd always remembered why he'd been with them—to make him forget.

But whenever he was with Ally, he could imagine that there was more to life than the problems that always waited for him outside the bubbles he created with the others. That there were ways to fix what ailed him, just as Ally fixed the problems of the world with her philanthropy.

That she could maybe fix him, too.

Tossing down his razor, he washed the cream from his face. There was no fixing him. He'd been born a player, inherited his personality from his father, and that was that.

But what would his dad do if Jeremiah brought someone like Ally home?

The rain on the roof paced his thoughts. Would being with someone of worth reflect on him in some way? And wouldn't it be damned nice to ditch all this bull about competing with his dad in the pleasing-women department by showing everyone that he, Jeremiah Barron, had risen above all that?

Roughly, he wiped his face with a towel, then pulled on another pair of jeans and a casual T-shirt. He went downstairs for breakfast, which was usually laid out buffet-style in the dining room.

Except for Ally's aunt Jessica, no one was up and about.

"Hi," she said, leaning back in her chair as she munched on a slice of bacon.

She had her hair in a high ponytail and was dressed in an oversize Longhorns sweatshirt and jeans. She didn't look a day over twenty-nine, even though Jeremiah knew that she was older than his own thirty-two years.

"Mornin'," he said, going for the banquet. "Where is everyone?"

"Who 'everyone'? Do you mean Ally?"

She lifted an eyebrow at him, and he merely went about grabbing a plate and filling it with some scrambled eggs.

"Everyone everyone," he said.

After a pause, she shrugged. "They're sleeping in, I expect. The guests are scheduled to leave today, and I'm sure they'll be taking off early because the rain has put the big kibosh on any riding or fishing they wanted to get in."

And the house would be relatively empty, leaving Ally with no pressing tasks.

Leaving her nearly alone with him.

Jeremiah shoveled some hash browns onto his plate. Then, sitting a few seats down from Jessica, he dug into his food.

"So," he asked casually, "what's on the schedule for you and your niece today?"

"I'm heading out later, after I explore the antiques they have in this joint. It'll almost be like shopping." She shot him a long gaze. "And as far as Ally goes, I believe she'll be playing hostess until the last guest leaves, then getting in some *alone* time."

Jessica clearly emphasized that one particular word.

She added, "Ally said something about sitting in the nook of one of the big bay windows around here and being a bookworm. There's something about rainy days and reading that she just loves."

Jeremiah smiled at the image of her getting cozy with a novel, happy and content, and he didn't even realize he'd reacted until he found Jessica staring at him.

He finished up his meal in a few more bites, then rose from the table. "Travel safe, then. It was good seeing you."

As he walked out of the room, he couldn't help thinking that Ally's aunt was still staring at him, wondering why he'd gotten that goofy smile on his face when she'd mentioned Ally curled up with a book.

Hell, he didn't know, either.

He spent the rest of the day in his room, waiting out the hours, using his laptop to catch up on business emails and checking in on the phone with the office. By the time he was done, it was late afternoon, but there was still one more matter to see to.

He called the family ranch to ask how his dad was doing.

"He's up in his room," said Millie, who was in charge of the household staff. "I looked in on him an hour ago, but he's been sleeping most of the day."

Jeremiah thanked her and disconnected, and sat in his chair a moment longer. Then, stifling a curse, he launched an internet search, reading about Alcoholics

Anonymous and forwarding the links to Tyler's and Chet's email addresses.

He shut down the computer, and it even seemed as if he was stowing away all the problems for now. Then he ventured out of his room. Surely guests would've left to get home in time for dinner; there'd been a long lull between the last batch of rain and now, as the drops began to tap against the windows again, so the weather would've provided some good traveling time.

He wandered, checking out those bay windows where Jessica had said Ally might be and, indeed, he found her sitting on the velvet cushions on one of them, nose deep in a hardbound leather book, her calico-skirted legs stretched out in front of her. Behind her, the rain trickled down the window, and she had a chenille blanket wrapped around her shoulders, thick cotton socks on her feet, comfy as could be.

Instinct told him not to press her on the personal front, so once again he turned to the subject of business.

He spoke softly, so as not to startle her.

"I'm going soon, Ally, and I don't want to leave without giving the subject of your Galveston property my best shot."

When she looked up, her eyes were wide, her lips parted.

Forget business.

He ached to bend down and kiss her until she moaned and clutched at him, showing him more than goosebumps on her arms. He wanted this woman more than he had any other, and it unnerved him that he didn't even know why.

In a quiet panic, he got himself together. Okay, so he

was smitten, but it would pass. His college sweetheart had taught him as much, but his father had made a good case for what DNA would provide for Jeremiah, too.

When Ally sedately grounded her feet on the floor and closed the book, he could've sworn that she closed her expression just as effectively, smiling politely at him as if they'd never had that discussion on the patio last night.

Just think about it, Ally….

She'd been hearing Jeremiah's voice in her head since last night, and she hadn't been able to *stop* thinking about what she wanted…and it had nothing to do with the business he'd come here to talk about, either.

Even as she'd sat here for hours, she'd found that she'd been reading the same words over and over. And now that he was here, she couldn't think at all, because her temples were drumming along with the voodoo cadence in the rest of her body.

Him, him, her pulse was saying, even while her brain was trying to cancel out every one of those beats.

She ran her gaze over him—a fantasy straight out of the ones she'd entertained last night after she'd gone to her room: Jeremiah Barron in blue jeans and a devil's grin, those blue eyes drawing her in with their lively spark.

"When are you leaving?" she asked, and it sounded so very nonsensical. But she didn't know what else to utter.

"I'll take off just as soon as you either tell me to go to hell or give me a sign that you're willing to bargain."

As cocky as always, he sat down next to her, a

buzzing space between them, even though he was about a foot away.

Her mouth was dry, so she swallowed, then said the most awkward thing she could've possibly ventured. "I guess it'd be tough for you to go back to San Antonio."

He paused, as if hardly believing she'd once again brought up a topic that would serve as a wedge.

Then he seemed to accept it. "I have to return sometime. Can't stay away and avoid real life forever. My family finally found that out, even though my dad and Uncle Abe tried for years to keep the scandal a secret. It was only when my uncle came down with cancer that it all emerged."

He was too close, and her heart was stuttering.

But she didn't move away from him. She liked that he seemed so different right now, more like that real guy she'd seen playing lassos with the children.

He continued, as if talking about this was inevitable. Or maybe a man like Jeremiah Barron was only using honesty to draw her in further....

"Uncle Abe knew he was dying," he said, "and he wanted Chet to have his rightful place in the family and business, so he told my dad that it was time for it all to see the light of day. He passed away knowing that my dad eventually did right by his son."

"I can't imagine what your family has been through, Jeremiah."

He didn't respond, but his expression said it all: the tightness of his jaw, the sudden shadows in his eyes.

She missed the usual twinkle. And it wasn't because she'd gotten used to the playboy. She just had the feeling that Jeremiah was truly a person who could make even the dourest of company lighthearted with his grin. That was a valuable talent, because everyone needed to be reminded that they could smile, even through the loneliest times.

When she looked back over at him, their mouths were only inches away.

The rain pattered against the window, her lips tingling with warmth.

"If you want to stay in the country for a little longer, I'm sure the Howards wouldn't mind," she said on a whisper.

"I'm sure they wouldn't."

And…even nearer now. Maybe she could be the one to close the distance, creating only a hush of space between them.

A tick of time.

A second that was poised to fall…

Ally closed her eyes, anticipating the press of his mouth on hers, a wicked trill grasping her heart—

As she felt his lips lightly brush over hers, a shock jolted her, one so strong that she drew back, sucking in a breath as her body flashed like it never had before.

Her pulse boomed, as if urging her to go on when it knew she shouldn't, when it knew that flirtation was one thing, but this?

It was another.

As she stood, her blanket slumped to the ground.

Her mouth still pounded while she walked away as fast as she could go. She'd dropped her book somewhere, but she wouldn't return to get it, even as Jeremiah said her name.

"Ally…"

He would be a mistake, and she wouldn't carry it with her into a new life with a *child,* for God's sake. She didn't need any attachments, even a temporary one, to a guy who had told her outright that he wasn't father material.

If there was a man in her life, he would have to be a constant.

She made it to her room, going inside, closing the door, leaning back against the wood, her common sense eventually coming back to her second by mortifying second.

She hadn't been thinking. But what scared her even more than that was that her body was punishing her now, churning in intimate places, keening for her to go back to him.

Would it have just been a kiss?

Half of her wanted to take a chance on being that one woman who saved Don Juan, to see where a kiss might lead, no matter what the consequences.

But she wouldn't let herself, and when she heard his boot steps coming down the hall, hesitating in front of her door, she held her breath.

It seemed like forever until he walked away.

Exhaling, she finally went to her desk, slumping into the chair. She grabbed a stack of papers—figures, numbers, all showing the success of the weekend—but she couldn't force herself to work.

Or to forget him.

She didn't know how long she sat there, but at some point, she could see that it was darker outside and raining harder than ever.

Idly, she reached for her phone, noticing only now that the message icon was on.

She accessed her voice mail, and it was as if fate had stepped in and guided her in the direction she needed to go.

And it wasn't out the door to find where Jeremiah had gone off to.

"Ally, this is Michele from the adoption service provider. I have some great news. We've got a birth mother who fell in love with your portfolio, and she wants to meet with you…."

Afterward, Ally held the phone to her chest as tears fell. This was really happening. And she'd made all the right decisions, even in the hallway.

Eventually, she dried her face and wrote a note to Jess, preferring to do that instead of having to listen to any more of her aunt's doubts about an adoption.

Then Ally went to Jess's room, slipped the paper under her door, said goodbye to the Howards and left the mansion, heading to California and the life that she'd been meant for.

"She's gone," Jessica said as Jeremiah stood in the dining room with her, where one last banquet had been laid out.

"Gone?"

He sounded as if he'd been smacked with a sledge-hammer to the head.

One more night. That's what he'd been hoping for. All it would've taken was another kiss. He should've still had a few hours to persuade Ally, too.

But here Jessica was, telling him that she wasn't here

anymore. She even seemed put out about it, too, for some reason.

He must have seemed bewildered, because Jessica got curious.

"Are you all right?"

Get a grip, Jer, he thought.

He called up his grin to pull him through. "She didn't say anything about leaving today."

"She had to get back to her place in California because..." Jessica pursed her lips together.

"Why?"

She blinked at the force of his tone. "It's just personal business. I have to leave it at that, Jeremiah."

Anger was rising in him. Punctured pride. That's what it had to be, because he'd been rejected—*royally* rejected—and word would get around about it soon enough. His friends would hear about it, then his family.

But there was another reason this injured him. It confirmed that he wasn't good enough. Not for Ally.

Maybe not for anyone. Ever.

Then he thought about his father—how he probably would not even react to Jeremiah's failure when all Jeremiah had ever wanted, really, was a response out of the man.

He couldn't figure out what made his feet move out of the room. Impulse. A rash sense of being put in his place by Ally yet again.

But something else, something he couldn't grasp, niggled at him, and Jeremiah abandoned it on his way to his room, taking out his smart phone, accessing his upcoming schedule.

He looked at what he would be able to cancel businesswise, what he could reschedule and what he couldn't avoid before going out of town. He was going to need at least a week and a half to get his affairs in order before taking any kind of vacation.

Then he dialed up his personal assistant, Rita.

"I've got a small research project for you," he said, going on to give her details about Ally…as well as what he knew about where she lived in California. Rita would do the rest.

He hung up, not having finished *any* business with Ally Gale, professional…

Or personal.

Chapter Four

Ally pushed back her wide-brimmed hat, lifting her face to the haze-veiled September coastal sun as its warmth spread over her garden, which was resplendent with herbs like rosemary and cilantro, plus vegetables like tomatoes, peppers, beans and lettuce.

It was so good to be home.

She'd been hoping for this kind of peace and quiet when she'd returned from Texas over a week and a half ago. Lord knew she had needed it most of all the day after her return, when she'd met with the birth mother of the child she planned to adopt.

Thank goodness the meeting had gone off without a hitch though. As the adoption services facilitator had sat nearby, Cheryl had interacted with Ally as if she really liked her, and Ally's nerves had been laid to rest as they had started to get to know each other.

From what the facilitator had previously told Ally,

the birth mother had taken her time in choosing the person she wanted her child to be with. But when she had come upon Ally and her portfolio, as well as her background information and glowing personal recommendation testimonials, she had made her decision.

Good thing, too, as Cheryl was due to give birth in only a couple more weeks.

As Ally watered the tomatoes with the garden hose, she couldn't help smiling. She was going to have what she wanted most soon: a baby, a family…

When she thought of having a husband to go along with the rest of it, she tried to shut down the longing. But it was impossible, because the rest of her became a tangle of heartbeats and adrenaline.

A man, to have and to hold, to be with and love.

The sensation of Jeremiah's lips skimming over hers came, unbidden…so soft and gentle, his mouth like a velvet stroke through the deepest and most intimate parts of her body….

She tried to shut that down, too, because she'd made her decision about Jeremiah Barron. He was the last thing a mother-to-be needed.

But there was just something else about him. Something that scared her—a powerful feeling she'd never felt before, not even with Marco. Yet a playboy like Jeremiah would only take advantage of her feelings and leave them like so much debris when he was done. She'd made a good choice in leaving him behind.

A woman's lilting voice came from behind her, bringing Ally out of her reverie.

"Well, there she is. You must've come out here right when the sun rose."

Ally hadn't noticed anyone approaching, but she should have heard Mrs. McCarter, the housekeeper who'd worked for Ally's parents ever since she could recall, limping with the aid of her cane. Behind her, there were rolling green, oak-laced hills, plus a small vineyard that rested in the near distance next to the country road.

"I thought you might have jet lag after getting in so late last night," Ally said, "so I thought I'd let you sleep in."

Mrs. McCarter had told Ally to call her by her first name, Marlene, now that Ally was an adult, even though she didn't because she thought it didn't sound right. As Mrs. McCarter sat down on a wooden bench, a breeze tickled the strands of short white hair that peeked out from beneath her yellow canvas hat. She folded both hands on the head of her mahogany cane and smiled and, like always, the humor traveled to her light brown eyes.

"Ah, the price of getting old," the woman said. "Sorry I drifted off before I could milk all the details out of you about your birth mother."

"I knew we'd have plenty of time to talk today and even long after that."

"So talk. Tell me *everything*."

For a second, Ally's mind snagged on the thoughts she'd been having about Jeremiah—a temptation she wasn't going to confess.

Taking up where they had left off last night, Ally said, "After meeting Cheryl, the adoption became much more real for me. It stopped being a dream, because there's a whole new batch of feelings that I didn't expect to be having."

Mrs. McCarter merely listened, just as she had on the phone when Ally had asked her to come out to the coast, to be here to keep her company. Jess would arrive in a few days, after she'd taken care of some of her own business. Ally's aunt still hadn't given her full blessing to the adoption, but at least this would be a step in the right direction, as Ally had made it clear that she was going through with it whether or not she had Jess's approval.

Ally shed her gardening gloves. "You should've seen the birth mother. She's not much more than a girl, even though she's twenty. She's got these big blue baby-doll eyes, and when she sat in the big wingback chair that the facilitator has in her office, she was just about swallowed up. She looked so *young,* even with a belly out to here."

Curving her hand through the air, Ally indicated the birth mother's swollen tummy. The gesture made her throat close up tight. If Marco had wanted her as a wife, *she* might've been just as pregnant as Cheryl by now.

She expected to feel pulled down by the thought, yet where there should've been sadness, there was only regret at having wasted her time on a man who'd preferred jetting around on business to settling down with her….

Before she realized what was happening, Jeremiah's face, with that charming grin and the twinkle in his eyes, covered everything, including the regret.

Ally erased the image from her mind, although there

was still something vibrating around the area of her heart.

Mrs. McCarter said, "How did this Cheryl seem to feel about letting her child go for adoption? Reluctant? Relieved?"

"Neither one, really. She told me that she never meant to get pregnant—not now and not in the future. She's a college student on scholarship, and she's got plans for a career as a lawyer." Ally didn't cotton to those sorts of ambitions, although she respected that Cheryl had them. "She knows that if she has a baby now, she'll have to give up all the opportunities she's worked so hard for. Plus, she said that she can't afford to raise a child the right way, and I think *that* trumped everything else."

"Her boyfriend won't support her and a baby?"

"There is no boyfriend." Ally stood, brushing the dirt from her jeans, then slipped her veggie- and herb-filled garden basket over her arm. "He was just a fling who didn't want any part of the pregnancy. When he was served papers for the adoption, he denied he was the father."

"Poor girl."

"Yeah. But she's not the sort who asks for pity. And she said that she doesn't want the child to pay for her mistakes."

"Well, it sounds like you both made the right decision. You were *meant* to have this baby."

Ally smiled gratefully at the older woman. She'd known that Mrs. McCarter would be a stabilizing force, just as when Ally was growing up she'd been there to offer a hug or two while Ally's parents went on weekend philanthropy trips. As the head of their household, she'd done more than just mind the books and run the Gales' personal business.

Mrs. McCarter leaned back on the bench, her hat shielding her skin from the sun. Her complexion was smooth, pale, parchment thin, soft as any grandmother's.

"Sounds to me," the older woman said, "that Cheryl thought very carefully about her options. There are just some women out there who don't feel the need to be a mother. I'm a prime example."

"You would've been a fantastic one."

"It wasn't in the cards." Mrs. McCarter winked at her. "I always had the best of arrangements. I would enjoy having fun with you, playing, taking you to the park and the like. But if you started to cry or fuss, I simply handed you off to your mom. I was quite pleased with the circumstances."

Ally laughed, helping the older woman off the bench, linking arms with her as they strolled on the path toward the house, which lorded it over the sweeping landscape with its modern glass-and-cedar sleekness. The surrounding shrubs could've used a good trim, but Ally was minding the landscaping budget, even thinking she would do some of it herself.

Being outdoors would be good for the soul, anyway.

Just as they approached the back door, Ally heard the roar of a truck coming up the long drive.

"Are you expecting company?" she asked Mrs. McCarter.

"At my age? You give me a lot of credit."

Laughing again, Ally let go of her friend and went

ahead toward the garage area, where a flatbed pickup was pulling in, the back brimming with...

Rosebushes?

Yes. Layer upon layer of red, yellow, white and pink petals spilling over the sides of their planters like a surreal fantasy.

And as if that wasn't surprising enough, the delivery man alighted from the truck, dressed in boots, jeans and a cowboy hat.

Ally could only stare as her mind raced to catch up with the sprint of her pulse.

Jeremiah Barron shut the truck's door, then took off his hat, tipping it to her.

"Mornin', Ally."

What the heck was he doing here?

Her foolish heartbeat took over, pounding so loudly that she couldn't hear much else, except his voice.

"I thought a little housewarming gift might be just the thing for you," he added.

Ally didn't know if he was talking about the roses or himself—a gift she would've surely sent back if she'd been given the option.

Jeremiah had thought long and hard about how to approach Ally again, but he wasn't used to pursuing a woman who didn't take much stock in his usual trade.

If he gave her diamonds, she would hand them right back.

If he bought her a flashy new car, she would never drive it.

And she had already refused the very idea of being

whisked off to a romantic destination when he'd suggested it back at the charity event in Texas.

So he'd gone simple by buying her some roses.

Okay—a *lot* of roses.

From the looks of her, it seemed as if he'd hit the nail on the head, too. Noting her elegant yet modest wide-brimmed straw hat, plus a flowing long-sleeved shirt over a white T and dirt-tinted jeans, he'd apparently caught her doing some gardening. The basket on her arm only proved his guess.

Down-to-earth, he thought, his belly clenching. She was so different from any of the others he'd wasted time with.

Different enough to matter?

No. Jeremiah had chased her here for no other reason than the usual—a challenge. A way to build up his pride, which had taken so many hits lately.

He motioned toward the roses. "I figured I could plant these for you. That way, they'll last."

She was shaking her head, obviously at a loss for words.

"Don't tell me you're not a rose kind of woman," he said.

When she took a step toward him, his heart jerked so hard that he thought it might've gotten yanked right out of him.

"You're not here for any housewarming," she said, keeping her voice low.

And he could see why, as an elderly woman limped toward them from around the side of Ally's home.

The dickens in him wanted to hurry up and tell Ally

that, indeed, he would like nothing better than to warm her house, but she was already talking again.

Two spots of color had settled on her cheeks. "I can't believe you came out here, Jeremiah."

He stopped joking around. "We had unfinished business. You left before any of it came to a close."

It was obvious that he meant more than just her Galveston property, because her cheeks pinkened even more deeply.

Was she remembering that kiss?

Before he'd come out here, as he'd taken care of final details before traveling, he hadn't been able to forget it—the way she'd smelled, like cherry blossoms. The way she'd made his mind spin, even before he'd touched his mouth to hers.

The way she'd run off, just as he was about to lose control and maybe even whisper something dangerous to her. Something soft and vulnerable that had no business escaping him.

He could see the flash of Ally's green-blue eyes, even from this near distance.

"We have no business," she said. "I told you that you should go through my managers if you want that property."

A tense moment boxed them in, as if they were the only two people in this area, this world. And in those few, dragged-out seconds, Jeremiah felt his heart expanding, becoming something so unfamiliar that fear pressed back against it out of sheer desperation.

He didn't have room for a heart that was any bigger than he meant it to be.

Breaking off their connected gaze, he turned to the

green pickup he'd rented back at the small airport by San Luis Obispo. The veins in his neck were thudding, as if something unexpected was playing him.

He unlatched the tailgate, scooping the first plastic planter full of roses into his arms. "Surely, by now, you've heard of my reputation—and I'm not talking about the one you read about on the gossip pages. When I set my mind on a business proposition, I go after it at the source. I don't mess around with middlemen."

"So this *is* all about the Galveston property."

He would go with that. "I'm serious about acquiring it, Ally. And I could make you an offer you wouldn't be able to refuse if you'd just hear me out."

For the first time, she seemed to give credence to his story. He could almost see the wheels turning in her head: selling the property to offset all the losses she'd suffered. Security in the profit she might make.

A sense of protection—of wanting to see that she was secure—assailed Jeremiah, and he had no idea where it came from.

"All I want to do is talk," he said.

While she looked into his eyes, as if to find the truth there, his chest seemed to open up, inviting her in even though it was the last thing he wanted.

Wasn't it?

She obviously read some less than noble intentions in him, and she glanced away, as if disappointed.

But why? Why expect much of anything from him except for the reputation he'd earned?

He didn't dare think that she saw more in him than other people did. Hell, even he didn't believe he was more than the tycoon playboy who journeyed from party to party.

"Where can I put these?" he asked softly, not realizing he was using that tone of voice until it had come out.

She hesitated, then pointed to the back of her home.

When she began walking in that direction, he followed like a damned puppy dog until he put down the planter.

A space had been cleared back here, near a Spanish tiled patio decorated with wrought-iron lawn furniture and benches. It was as if Ally had been planning a flower garden but hadn't gotten around to making it a reality yet.

He gestured to the distance, where, over the hills, a hint of the ocean broke through the haze.

"Perfect view," he said. "How big are you going to make this garden?"

"Nice sized." She gave a puzzled look to the rose planter he'd been holding. "I was actually thinking about roses—rows and rows of them, with gravel pathways."

Bull's-eye. Damn, he was good.

He tried to extend his streak. "I grew up with a garden like that, where you could walk through the lines of flowers." He remembered Florence Ranch, with the magnolias, azaleas and wisteria in the back of the big house. As a boy, he'd run through its mazes. As an adult, he'd taken drinks back there, figuring out how to navigate other mazes, like those he encountered in business.

Ally was a maze, too, he thought, and he wasn't sure which way to go with her.

Or what might be at the end.

But who was he kidding? She would provide the same conclusion all the other women had—a sense of triumph at a conquest well done. Satiation, carnal and temporary.

He started to walk back to the pickup for more roses, but her voice stopped him.

"Despite everything, I just want to thank you for the thought. The roses, I mean."

Was she coming around? "You're welcome."

"It was just a shock to see you here."

"You should've known that I wouldn't be content with where we left matters."

He didn't say whether he meant the Galveston property or something else, and he could see a battle playing out over her otherwise serene face.

It didn't make him feel good to be the cause of such confusion, either. For some reason, he felt dirtied, as if he should be better around her.

"Ally," he said.

But she stopped him there, too.

"I was serious when I said you should go through my business managers. All the roses in the world can't change my mind about that. Not about…anything."

It was like an arrow through the heart, because he knew that she really wasn't talking about the Galveston property anymore.

She left him standing there, walking away from him across the patio and going through the sliding back door, closing it with a final thud.

The sound reawakened every reason he'd come out here in the first place—to win, to show her and everyone else that he wasn't irrelevant. That he could matter.

He went back to the pickup and finished unloading his housewarming gift.

Jeremiah had been shut out too many times by his father. He'd been put at the back of the line, first with Tyler and now with Chet.

And he would be damned if it was going to happen again with Ally.

Ally had sequestered herself in her master bedroom, taking a shower, then putting on a sundress. She wasted so much time that she thought Jeremiah might've already unloaded the roses and left her to deal with them.

After all, she'd made it clear that she expected him to leave.

As she brushed out her damp hair, her inner clock ticked away. Was it safe to venture out?

The woman in the mirror of the antique vanity table stared back at her, wide-eyed, cheeks flushed. She looked…colorful. As if thoughts of Jeremiah animated her more than usual.

She tossed the brush into a drawer and used a hair band to fix her hair into a low, floppy, casual bun. Surely he was gone by now.

As for the gift he'd given her… Well, she was certainly grateful and a bit stunned by it—heck, she *had* planned to put roses in that same patch of land—but she knew that Jeremiah's presents no doubt came with strings attached….

She emerged from her room and went to the kitchen,

going toward the vegetable basket she'd set on the wooden island in the middle of the room.

Then she heard laughter.

Wrinkling her brow, she looked around. It didn't take long to find where the sounds were coming from as she went to the patio window, where she found an unwelcome sight.

Jeremiah sat at the wrought-iron table with Mrs. McCarter, who was giggling like a young girl at some joke he'd obviously made. They had iced teas in front of them, as if it was happy hour.

Why hadn't she seen this coming? Of course Mrs. McCarter would've introduced herself to him, and of course he would've charmed the lashes off of her.

Ally was certain that her friend wouldn't have told him about the adoption plans—she'd sworn Mrs. McCarter to discretion—but she wondered what else Jeremiah might've wheedled out of her by now.

She slid open the glass door, catching the attention of the pair.

Mrs. McCarter lifted her iced tea. "Join us, Ally. It's a beautiful day."

"Yeah," Jeremiah said, grinning, his cowboy hat on the chair next to him, leaving his hair boyishly ruffled. "Join us."

"May I speak with you?" Ally said to Mrs. McCarter, ignoring him altogether.

The woman glanced at her silver watch. "I should get my duff up anyway if I'm going to help Ally with our late lunch." She turned to Ally. "What are we having? Vegetable sandwiches and that French cheese you picked up from the market?"

Ally knew just where this was going, and she motioned for Mrs. McCarter to get that duff of hers inside.

As her friend obliged, Jeremiah focused on the view again. Near him, all his roses waited in their planters like an army of thorns in her side.

After Ally shut the patio door, Mrs. McCarter said, "What a wonderful young man. I didn't know he was a friend of yours."

"He's not."

"But…"

"He's a business shark, and he's interested in the old Galveston resort. I've told him that I'm not up to dealing with him."

Mrs. McCarter didn't need to know the rest.

"Weren't you thinking seriously about selling the property? It's out of use, anyway."

"Yes, but… Not to him."

"Because…?"

"Because he's not the type of man I, personally, would do business with. I still have a few people on payroll for that."

"Oh?"

Mrs. McCarter looked doubtful about that, as if Jeremiah Barron was just the kind of guy who was worthy of Ally's trust.

"Please tell me that you didn't invite him to stay for lunch," Ally said.

The other woman shrugged.

"He can't stay."

"It would be rude to take back the invitation, especially after he brought all those roses."

Clearly, Mrs. McCarter was under his spell. Perfect. What would it take for him to go?

Ally watched him through the patio door—how he'd stretched his long, jeans-clad legs in front of him, as if he was completely at home. How well his body—broad shoulders, lean hips, nice butt and all—fit so well into her chair.

Too comfortable. Too…

Then it hit her.

She knew what would scare a playboy off.

"Would you do me a favor and wash the vegetables?" she asked Mrs. McCarter. "I'll be back inside shortly to do the rest."

The older woman gave Ally a measuring glance, but she went to the kitchen anyway.

Ally opened the door and stepped through. First, she would lead up to her plan, fooling him with kindness. Then…

Bam.

When she sat down in the chair that Mrs. McCarter had vacated, Jeremiah got that rogue's grin again, as if he thought he'd come one step closer to winning her over.

Even while Ally's body filled with buzzing shocks, just from being this close to him, she calmed herself down, relaxing back into her chair. She could see out of the corner of her eye how he grew a little cautious at her sudden change of attitude.

"So you're staying for lunch?" she asked.

"If that's fine with you."

"Oh, sure, as long as you don't mind a lot of girl talk between me and Mrs. M."

A sideways smile swiped his mouth. "Sounds fine to me."

"Good. It's just that a lot has been happening with me."

"I imagine. Settling into a new home must take up a lot of your time. Is that why you hightailed it back out here after the charity event?"

He was prodding her into talking about that kiss, but she would be damned if she'd give in.

"Sure, the house is one of the reasons I left in such a hurry that day." Before he could say anything, she added, "There was a lot of work to get done around here, with putting final touches on the rooms—one in particular that needs extra attention."

"Which one?"

"The nursery."

At that last word, Jeremiah froze, his grin fading.

"Nursery?" he asked.

"Yes." She put on her own smile, sweet as could be, preparing to force his hand. "I'm adopting a baby."

Chapter Five

Baby?

As the words sank in, Jeremiah's vision fuzzed, breaking his view of Ally into a puzzle with all the beautiful pieces scattered.

Kids were scary enough, but when he thought of *babies,* he pictured little helpless bundles who cried all night and looked up at you with wide, innocent stares that said, "I depend on you, and only you. Love me. Be responsible for me."

Babies.

Good God. He could put together million-dollar deals at the drop of a hat, but babies scared him witless. They needed guidance, good modeling. They were nothing to be taken lightly.

Not like this game he'd been playing with Ally.

As if things weren't complicated enough, Jeremiah

also realized that when she left the Howards' ranch it wasn't because of that kiss they'd shared.

She'd had an adoption to take care of out here.

While he shifted in his chair, his gaze snapped into focus on Ally, who sat across from him, angling her head as if she'd witnessed some sort of truth in Jeremiah.

"Did I surprise you?" she asked.

If he didn't know better, he might've said she'd put forth the question with a certain amount of satisfaction.

"Yeah. Kind of." But then he recalled the look on her face that he'd seen back on the Howards' ranch, when she'd been watching the children outside. "Or maybe I *shouldn't* be surprised. You're meant to have kids. A family. It's just that…"

"You didn't expect me to jump the gun before I got married." It was as if she'd put her usual shield back up—polite, kind, but still remote. "If you wanted children, wouldn't you do the same? You strike me as someone who goes out and gets what he wants, too."

He had to admire her gumption. But…

A baby.

Jeremiah had the urge to reach for his hat, say farewell, then go on his merry way. It was one thing to cuddle up to a single woman who didn't offer too many complications, but a mother-to-be?

He steeled himself for the inevitable instinct to run.

Waited for it.

And waited.

Yet, here he still was. Even odder, there was something else taking him over.

Curiosity. About her. About why she *needed* a child

in her life. About why she thought this was going to complete her when nothing else had.

How had she found answers when he couldn't? What did she know about how to get them that he just couldn't figure out?

"Why?" he asked. "What made you decide to do this?"

Ally seemed taken off guard, as if she'd expected him to blaze out of here at the mere mention of a baby.

"I guess I'm just a nester," she said. "A quiet life is all I've ever wanted, with family. With people who'll spend the rest of their lives with me."

"You're going to retire here, in the country?"

"With pleasure."

Jeremiah tried to picture himself doing the same, getting away from the high life—all the things that had kept him going during the scandal, all the pretenses he'd been able to hide behind. But he felt bereft. Bare.

Truly and very much alone.

Yet, what if there was someone else with him? Someone who mattered…?

He could hardly believe what was running through his mind, but there it was, and he let it linger, just for a frightening moment.

Two moments.

Then he said, "I get why you'd want to have a baby, but…adoption?"

When Ally lowered her gaze, he got a hint.

"Marco," he said. "Do you think he was your last chance at having a family? And you're taking matters into your own hands?"

She just sat there for a second, and he began to doubt she would ever answer him.

But then she said, "I'm optimistic enough to believe that there will be other chances. It's just that I genuinely felt that there was a child out there *now,* somewhere. Someone who needs a home. This world is full of children who need. I should know, because I was adopted."

Something swelled in Jeremiah—the sense that, at one time, she'd been a little lost, too, just as he was now. The difference was that someone had taken her in.

Her candor surprised him, and it must have done the same to her, because she sat straighter in her chair.

"I'm not fooling myself though," she said. "It's not going to be easy. There'll be more sacrifices for me than just withdrawing from the social scene. Even now, I've got a thousand things to contend with, like the home inspection and background checks that the state will be doing on me after the baby's born." She smiled. "Weird—you'd think that they'd be doing those *before* the adoption, but that's how it goes with an independent service. I've been childproofing the house like mad for the visit."

Okay, now it seemed as if she was laying it on thick, as if she knew that the more he heard, the more uncomfortable he would get.

"When are you officially going to be a mom?" he asked, despite the urge to leave.

"Officially?" She got a dreamy smile on her face, and it grabbed Jeremiah. Right in the chest, too, where he felt pulled, captured by a tug that he couldn't define.

A tug he wanted to feel with his own family.

"The birth mother's due to have the baby pretty soon," Ally said. "But as far as I'm concerned, I'm already a mom." Her voice choked up. "To think—in just a short time, I'm going to have someone who really gives my life some meaning."

Warmth suffused him, and he wished it would stay beyond this moment while he sat here, watching as a happy glow captured her skin, her gaze. But a coldness—the *reality*—crept up on him. He was only getting a secondhand high from her own joy.

It wasn't his.

Not knowing what to make of the emotions scrambling around inside of him, Jeremiah fetched his hat from the seat next to him.

"Thanks for the drink," he said, standing and gesturing to the iced tea. "And just so you know, I won't just be leaving those roses there. I'll make some calls and see that they get planted."

At the prospect of his departure, relief took over her expression. It bruised him in places that he'd never thought vulnerable.

Best to get out of here. Best to find another distraction, one far less complex than Ally Gale and her upcoming family.

"Jeremiah?" she said as he began to walk away, sliding his hat onto his head.

He glanced at her, his gut wrenched by how the sunlight shone over her light hair, by the grace of her heart-shaped face and the clarity of her gaze.

But the thing was, when they locked gazes, she looked just as affected as he was. He could've sworn it,

especially when she glanced away, as if she didn't want
him to see.

"I appreciate your housewarming gift," she finally
said. "It was thoughtful of you."

He paused, not wanting to leave—not after what he'd
just witnessed in her.

But then he remembered the baby, and that made the
leaving easy.

He took the long, white-fence-lined roads leading
away from Ally's property until he came to Highway
101, which overlooked the ocean on its way to destina-
tions unknown.

But, for some reason, Jeremiah didn't take the on-
ramp. No, instead he drove toward the first decent hotel
he saw—a Victorian building with stained-glass windows in Pismo Beach, overlooking the ocean.

He had no idea what he was doing, sticking around.
Maybe because he really did want that Galveston property from Ally.

Yet, he knew that the real estate had always just been
an excuse to be near her.

Either way, he checked into a room where he could
hear the waves roar softly, accompanied by the cries
of seabirds. The sunlit water reminded him of Ally's
eyes—the glow he'd seen in them as she'd talked about
having a family.

About finding something of value.

He grabbed his phone from his jeans pocket and dialed his brother Tyler's number. It was just the first of
a few calls he should make—this one now, then to his
assistant in the Barron Group's office.

When Tyler answered, Jeremiah could hear the sounds of a whinnying horse and activity in the background.

"Busy?" Jeremiah asked.

"Just in the stables."

He'd obviously caught his brother at work on his horse rescue operation, but it didn't sound as if Ty was in any hurry to hang up.

"I thought I should check in," Jeremiah said, leaning on the balcony rail as a family walked past on the shore, barefooted, hand in hand as their youngest kid darted in and out of the waves.

"Why? Where are you?"

"Pismo Beach, California. Business errand."

"As usual."

Silence stretched while Jeremiah mentally beat around the bush, not wanting to ask about their father and wanting to at the same time.

He finally gave in. "Should I be in any hurry to come back?"

"If you're asking about Dad, then I don't know what to tell you. Chet and I have talked with each other until we're blue in the face, and we still don't know what to do about him."

Chet, their new brother.

Just the mention of him was enough to resurrect the isolation that gaped inside Jeremiah. The petty half of him thought, *Hell, let the new guy and Tyler handle this on their own since they're so tight now.*

But the other half?

It wanted to be in Texas, too, a part of the solution. Being with the others instead of looking in from the outside.

Tyler added, "We've been talking about an intervention. I don't know at what point a person becomes a real alcoholic, but Dad's sure on his way, and he's not going to go into a treatment facility on his own."

"You know how he'd react to that. He'd say we're all ganging up on him and he'll drink himself silly afterward, just to show us who's boss."

"You're right."

Frustration stiffened Jeremiah's spine. Anger at a stubborn, egotistical, selfish father who expected so much out of his family—and who treated them like minor planets that merely orbited him.

He watched the family on the beach walking away, their laughter growing fainter and fainter. "I'll contact a few professionals I found on the internet, just so we can get good advice."

"Chet and I got those links you sent, and we followed up on them already."

Oh.

Once again, a day late and a dollar short.

"Jer," Tyler said. "What you've already done was a big help, okay? Just get your business taken care of in California. We'll be waiting for you here."

"All right."

And they said goodbye.

Though Jeremiah had signed off, he felt as if he was being pulled toward Texas while he was still actually here, in a place where he'd seen something in Ally today—something that encouraged him, told him that he was missing clues that would lead to answers, and he could find them if he only looked hard enough.

Something that told him he mattered more to her than she was letting on.

He watched the water and let himself sink into the green and blue.

Let himself drown in what he kept telling himself was only his latest distraction and nothing more than that.

The morning sun peeked through the nursery window of Ally's home, shining through the sheer pink curtains she was holding against the frame.

"What do you think?" she asked Mrs. McCarter as the older woman sat in a chair, crocheting a christening cap. She was near the pewter Venetian-style crib that had just been delivered—a decently priced piece of furniture that would be here when the baby became old enough to need it, although it would be a while. Until then, a matching cradle had been set up in Ally's room, near her bed, where her baby would sleep near and dear to her.

"Pink isn't going to work if the child isn't a girl," the older woman said.

Ally held up a swath of blue instead. "That's why I'm prepared. But I suppose I can't settle on a color until the baby is born since Cheryl didn't want to know the sex."

Mrs. McCarter narrowed her eyes at the blue curtain as Ally tested it. "You can use a neutral decoration scheme…and pick a bunch of names from both sexes. Any decisions on that yet?"

"I'm still working on it." Ally toyed with a yellow curtain swatch. For a boy, she couldn't decide between her father's name, Robert, or something more fun, like Luke, as in Skywalker. She was a total closet *Star Wars* geek. That's why she'd also been thinking of Leia for a girl. But Ally had told everyone, including Michele her facilitator, that if the baby was female she wanted Caroline, her mom's name. Besides, she liked that old song "Sweet Caroline," too.

"Maybe," Mrs. McCarter said, "you should ask around for name ideas. I think that Jeremiah fellow might have a few when he comes back to plant those roses."

Ally sent the evil eye to her friend. Mrs. McCarter had been bringing up his name every chance she got, teasing Ally mercilessly, even though Ally had tried to explain yet again that he was just here for business reasons. The roses had only been a way to ingratiate himself to them.

Mrs. McCarter shrugged, her crocheting needle at a standstill. "I saw what I saw when I was watching you two from the kitchen window yesterday."

"You were supposed to be prepping lunch."

"It was far more entertaining to see you acting as if you don't have a care in the world for him."

"Now, Mrs.—"

Mrs. McCarter brooked no bull. "I've seen you grow up, Allison, and never before have I noticed that kind of flush on you when you're around a man. I'm only wondering why you're not giving him an opportunity to be nice to you."

"There're so many reasons that I'm not even going to start." Ally shoved the fabric samples into a bag on the floor. "Besides, if you knew anything about Jeremiah Barron, you'd realize that he's not..."

She was just about to say "daddy material." But then she recalled her gut instinct when she'd seen him playing with those children on the Howards' ranch. He'd been so natural around them—so much so that she'd pictured him with a family of his own someday, after he came around to recognizing he was capable of more than being a playboy.

Ally couldn't stand not to finish out her thought. "If you knew him, you'd realize his heart's not into any kind of commitment outside of business. That's not what I'm looking for in anybody I should happen to date in the future. If there's going to be any man in my life, he'll have to be good for the baby."

"He sure didn't look at you like some fly-by-nighter, Ally."

"You're just saying that because he charmed you silly. That's what he does. He's incredibly good at it, and you're just his latest victim. Besides, he's not coming back to plant those flowers."

Putting an end to the conversation, Ally went about combing through a book of wallpaper samples to see what she liked most for a nursery theme: bunnies? Balloons? Puppy dogs?

But, sometime along the line, she heard noises outside—the sound of a truck, then digging.

Obviously, Jeremiah had made good on his promise to get someone here to take care of the roses. And he'd given the landscaper some instructions so he could get started right away.

Disappointment pinched her, although there was no

reason for it. She'd known Jeremiah wouldn't be back. She'd rattled him with her baby stories.

Why should she care though?

When Ally went to the patio door and peered out, intending to greet the landscaper, she took a step back. Then she looked out again, her mouth agape.

Jeremiah *was* out there, digging away in her garden with a shovel, wearing a T-shirt and jeans that clung to his lean body in every libido-teasing place she could've named.

She moved out of sight so he wouldn't see her, but she couldn't purge the vision of him in that white cotton shirt, already damp with sweat, showing the flushed hint of skin underneath, the firmness of broad shoulders, a muscled back, a trim waist.

Low in her belly, she felt a twirl of lust that sent fantasy into motion: running her hands over that back and those arms. Resting her cheek against him, wrapping her arms around him so her fingers could travel the ripples of muscle over his stomach.

Then Ally realized that she wasn't breathing, and she drew in some air.

She would have to get rid of him, before she did something stupid, before she lost her head and gave in to those tiny voices that said, "Why not just this once…?"

Mrs. McCarter came into the living room, then went to the patio door while leaning on her cane. "Well, look at that."

"Not a word."

The older woman offered a sassy smile, then opened the door.

Oh, brother.

"Hello, there," she said to Jeremiah.

If you can't beat them, Ally thought, *join them.* For now.

She came out onto the patio, too, where the sun was shining in the sky, breaking through the coastal mist.

Jeremiah had already tipped his hat to Mrs. McCarter, and when he saw Ally, he grinned.

I'm ba-ack, his smile said.

"Changed my mind," he said. "I figured I could use the workout."

She tried not to look at his muscles again. He no doubt worked out plenty to get those biceps.

Mrs. McCarter held a hand over her heart. "So nice."

Ally kept her tongue. Jeremiah saw the effort, too, because when he put his hat back on, he laughed a little.

"Water?" Ally asked, thinking that it might put him at maximum efficiency.

The sooner she got Jeremiah out of here, the better. He was like a rolling boulder that she couldn't stop, so she would just let him finish without standing in his way and getting run over.

"Water would be good," he said.

Mrs. McCarter chimed in. "We'll fix some lunch, too, seeing as you weren't able to stay yesterday."

"Even nicer," he said.

But Ally had already gone back into the house, heading for the kitchen. She would bring out the food, then leave him to it, only because she suspected that visiting with him would just encourage him to keep *on* dogging her.

When she opened the fridge and started tossing out random things for lunch, Mrs. McCarter interrupted.

"Let me take care of this. I'm the one who invited him."

Ally's first instinct was to insist on helping, but Mrs. McCarter didn't like being reminded that she used a cane. To her way of thinking, she moved just as well these days as she had before she'd slowed down.

Letting her friend play hostess, Ally went to work in the nursery.

Much later—hours and hours—she emerged after deciding on a bunny-rabbit motif and ordering what she would need online for delivery. She also managed to put together a diaper-changing stand by herself, too.

By now, it wasn't only past lunchtime, but the sky had darkened enough for dinner to be served.

Surely he would be gone.

But when she checked, Jeremiah was still working away under the lights of the citronella tiki torches that lined the patio. While Mrs. McCarter set the table with dinnerware and drinks, he stayed hip-deep in roses. He'd planted them in a way that allowed for gravel lanes, like a small maze.

In spite of herself, Ally admired his work through the kitchen window, then pulled herself away. She would just send him a thank-you card.

Mrs. McCarter must have seen her wandering around in the kitchen, and she came inside.

"So," she said, smiling at Ally. "What do you say to some cocktails and then we'll talk about dinner? He's worked hard out there."

"I know he has, but..."

She was at her wits' end, feeling as if her troops had deserted her for the dark side.

"You know I'm not going to sit down with you," Ally finally said. "If I do, he'll *never* leave."

Mrs. McCarter sighed. "It's up to you, Allison."

She went back out to the table and, boy, did Ally feel rude—and about ten years old, besides.

But she had to stick to her guns.

She grabbed a bag of carrots from the fridge, electing to go back to work in the nursery. By the time the sky had deepened to true darkness, curiosity got the better of Ally, and she went to the patio door yet again, seeing Jeremiah and Mrs. McCarter eating some kind of salad and laughing together, as usual.

What—was he planning to move in?

Ignoring him clearly wasn't working, so she had to end this once and for all.

When Ally came outside, Jeremiah and Mrs. McCarter looked at her.

The older woman, as subtle as ever, reached up her arms, yawning. "My. What time is it?"

Jeremiah didn't move from his chair as Mrs. McCarter rose from her seat, fetching her cane, then passed Ally as she made her way inside.

Ally folded her arms over her chest against the night air, which had grown cool. She saw the rose garden, so neat and tidy, with graveled paths amidst the burst of petals, and her defenses lowered a bit.

He *had* put a lot of work into his gift. Not even Marco had made such a nice gesture to her in the months they'd been together....

Jeremiah's gaze was on the sky, his cowboy hat

hanging on the next chair, leaving his hair in that endearing mess that always seemed to work its way into Ally's heart.

End this now, she thought. *Get him out of here before...*

She thought of that kiss, and her skin came alive, caressed by memory, by the need for more.

"Ally," he said quietly.

Too quietly. It was a tone she hadn't heard Jeremiah use much, just during those moments when he seemed to drop the playboy act and reveal something underneath it all. Of course, he always returned to form.

"Jeremiah," she said, "I appreciate all you've done. But you've got to go."

"I know that."

She blinked, wondering if she'd heard him correctly. At the same time, a sinking sensation traveled from her heart to her stomach.

More disappointment?

"But before I leave," he said, "I'd like you to sit with me. Just for a minute or two."

Had he come to terms with reality?

Would he finally leave if she did this one little thing?

It seemed worth the gamble, so Ally sat down next to him, never even thinking that the terms just might be all his.

Chapter Six

Jeremiah had bided his time all day, betting that Ally would, at some point, come out, even if it was just to send him on his way.

And, sure enough, here she was, next to him, the light from the stars silvering her long, unbound hair, driving him crazy with the desire to feel it flow through his fingers.

But he'd also stayed around because he wanted more from her, although Lord knew what it was. Maybe he would figure it out before he left.

Or maybe he never would.

"Mrs. McCarter told me that you've been working in the nursery all day," he said. "She mentioned something about bunnies."

"Bunnies are cute for a baby room."

She was still on guard, and the fighter within Jeremiah—the one that had kept him going every time he'd felt shut out while his dad had taken Tyler under his wing—raged on. The fighter made Jeremiah want to make Ally see him as more than some pain in the ass, even if she'd already dismissed him just as thoroughly as everyone else had during his lifetime.

He felt her glance at him, and *his* skin prickled to goosebumps this time.

"It's not that I think you're a bad guy," she finally said. "It's just that I need certain things for my baby."

"Like stability. And people around here who'll be good influences."

She nodded. "Even back in Texas, I knew I'd be starting a new life, and—"

"That's why you left. I get it, Ally."

He wanted to ask what might've happened in Texas if she hadn't been planning to adopt, but he wasn't sure he wanted to hear the answer.

As soon as he realized that he was gripping his water glass, he loosened his hold.

Now Ally seemed to relax a bit, too, probably because he wasn't selling her a bill of goods anymore, pretending like he'd come out here to woo her for a business deal.

If he had any brains whatsoever, he would cut his losses and run. By contacting her business managers, as she'd suggested, he could even save face, making everyone think that he *had* indeed visited to talk her into a sweet deal on the Galveston property and that he'd closed it.

But it wasn't enough.

Why? Why couldn't he just let this go?

She tilted back her head, fixing her gaze on the sky,

as if she was trying to think of a graceful way to brush him off and out of here.

Jeremiah bought more time with her by motioning toward the sky. "You going to do a lot of stargazing out here?"

"It seems a fine place for it."

"That's the first thing I'd do. Back on Florence Ranch, when I was on vacation from boarding school, I had a telescope, and I used it near the gardens. Since the ranch is a bit distant from the city lights, the skies were clearer."

"Were you a science geek?" She was giving him an odd glance.

He shrugged, the expert at hiding a lot of deeper things about himself. The king of deception. "I wouldn't call myself a *geek*. I only had an interest. Besides, it got me out of the house most nights."

He didn't add that it had been much easier for him to look at something far off than to deal with the sight of his dad fawning over Tyler, molding him, paying so much attention to him that it sent an unmistakable message: there wasn't time for Jeremiah. He wasn't worth the investment.

Pushing the thought away, he said, "I bought a high-powered telescope and everything. Once, Ty called me a nerd. I think I was about ten, so I didn't realize how successful nerds are in the outside world and I gave him a shiner."

Privately, his father had laid into Jeremiah for it, too, protecting his precious Ty, yet never letting Tyler himself know just how much he cared for him. Jeremiah might have been the only one to see that Eli loved his oldest son best. Then again, Dad *had* seemed to realize it, holding that over Jeremiah's head in a sort of silent triumph, as if it would somehow push Jeremiah into being as good as Ty.

"After that," Jeremiah said, "I didn't use the telescope much anymore."

He hadn't meant to fish for sympathy, but Ally was watching him with a soft gaze anyway. It was the last thing he wanted from her, and he downed a gulp of water, hoping to break the moment.

It worked, because she offered a casual comment.

"At least you were a nerd with a good right hook."

Jeremiah laughed and Ally smiled, too.

Yeah, he could make this last.

He used his finger to trace a pattern in the sky.

"During the right time of the year, I always seem to find the archer first. I guess because it's my sign."

"Sagittarius is mine, too," she said, before pressing her lips together, as if she regretted adding to the conversation.

"That's the last sign I thought you'd be."

"Why?"

"It has to do with fire, right?" And she was all coolness and blue, just like the green-tinted azure of her eyes. "I would've guessed you were an Aquarius."

"You would've guessed wrong." She said it as if there was a lot about her that she hid, just like he did. And based on how she'd surprised him with the baby news, Jeremiah supposed that she was just as good at keeping things to herself as he was.

He pointed to the sky again, connecting a cluster of stars that formed a stringed instrument. "And there's

Lyra. The lyre. There's a good story behind every constellation, and this one has to be in the top five."

"Hermes invented the lyre, right? At least, according to the Greeks."

So she was an undercover nerd, too.

A warm patch swirled inside Jeremiah, as if it was forming its own pattern. He had no idea what it would be though.

"He pulled a cow gut across a tortoise shell or something, then gave it to Apollo," Jeremiah said. "Then *he* gave it to Orpheus, and he learned how to play it so well that he charmed the tar out of anyone who heard him. Of course, that's when he went down to the underworld to bring back his dead wife."

Jeremiah kept staring at Lyra, remembering how he'd often gone to his room after looking at the stars, reading up on astronomy and the Greek myths behind all those constellations out there. "Orpheus played that lyre for Hades to convince him to let Eurydice, his wife, go. Hades was so touched that he gave his okay, but only if Orpheus didn't look back at her during the return trip home."

Ally didn't interrupt, and he wasn't sure if it was because she didn't know the end of the story or if it was because she was thinking about how tragically it had all turned out.

"But he did take a peek behind him," Jeremiah said, "just as he was emerging into the sunlight and…"

He made a *poof* motion with his hand.

In the resulting silence, he thought about the bigger meaning of this story, about how looking back could damage a person.

Take his college sweetheart, for instance. She'd been a nice girl who was so curious about being with a bad boy that she hadn't been able to help herself. But he'd loved her—at least, that's what he'd thought—and he'd tried hard to change.

Tried but failed. He'd given into his nature one stupid night at an out-of-town party. But he'd still put his heart out there for her afterward, saying he would never stray again, and he had meant it.

Yet, after that, she'd never trusted him. She'd looked back when she could've looked forward, to their future, and it had destroyed everything, including Jeremiah's courage to offer his heart to anyone else again.

After that, he knew that every woman would look back at his history, and rightly so. And when she did, *he* would also look behind him, just to see if she was still with him. That's when he would find that she'd disappeared—just as thoroughly as Orpheus's wife—a woman who was never meant to be with him forever, anyway.

Jeremiah supposed that this was only one of the many reasons that he'd decided to live for the moment, to take what he had before it all *poof*ed away.

Ally had been sitting still, clearly affected by the story, so softhearted, so empathetic, and as the moon and stars shone down on her, Jeremiah had never wanted to kiss any woman so badly in his life.

Knowing there might never be another opportunity with her—not with a child involved—he decided to live for *this* moment.

He leaned toward Ally, who only had time to suck

in a stunned breath before he pressed his mouth against hers, fully.

Softly.

But in that softness, there was also a hint of insistence, and when she didn't resist him, he slid his hand to the back of her neck, feeling her smooth skin and the fall of hair that rained over his knuckles. The sensuality of it all—the warmth of her skin versus the coolness of her hair—drizzled into Jeremiah, coating him with a longing so strong that he never wanted to let go of her.

What was so different about this woman that kept him making a fool of himself and coming back for more?

Under his lips, she made a small, needful sound, and that pierced Jeremiah with an ache that only sharpened. He deepened the kiss, brought it to a longing draw that allowed him to taste her, smell her, get dizzy on her as she responded by latching her fingers onto his shirt.

She pulled on the material, bringing him closer, and he wound his other arm around her waist, urging her against him.

Ally seemed to melt, boneless, all heat.

She wanted him. No matter what she did, how remote and disinterested she seemed, this kiss wasn't lying.

Desperate for breath, he skimmed his mouth down her chin, to her throat, where he rested against the wild thud of her vein.

Yes, it said, punching in quick time, poking holes in him that felt like bright bursts of light. *Yes, yes, yes...*

As she breathed against his temple, his hands itched to roam up her body, to cup her breasts and circle his thumbs around the centers of them until she was doing more than panting.

That's what a playboy would do—take advantage, get all he could while the getting was good.

But, when around her, that man faded to the background, letting someone else emerge, someone Jeremiah hadn't seen since those days of vulnerability and broken dreams in college.

And that man ended the kiss, easing her back into her chair.

She seemed just as thwarted as he was, but in his gut, he knew he was doing the right thing. He was going toward a better place, and she'd been the one to start him off in that direction.

Before he changed his mind, he took up his hat, put it on his head, then stood.

"Good night, Ally," he said.

He walked toward his pickup, and even though he knew he shouldn't, he looked back at her.

Much to Jeremiah's shock, Ally was still there, her fingers on her lips, as if she'd never been kissed that way in her life.

His veins pumping with a lightness he hadn't felt in a long time, Jeremiah sauntered the rest of the way to his truck, wondering how the hell he was going to stay away from Ally Gale now.

The next afternoon, Ally was still in a daze from that kiss.

Her lips were still humming, as if Jeremiah was close enough to kiss her again. His scent, earthy and manly from the work he'd been doing, had lit up a primal need in her body, which was still on fire. It was as if the mere touch of him had the power to travel into her, abrading every cell with pleasure when he'd made his move—one that she'd fallen right into because she hadn't expected it.

But she hadn't exactly refused him. Where had the good girl gone? Where was the responsible woman who didn't want any bad influences around her?

"Ally?"

She blinked, everything coming into focus at once: the chirp of birds, the table in front of her, the trellises surrounding the outdoor tables of the café where she had invited Michele, her facilitator, and Cheryl, the birth mother. She had just wanted to thank both of them for everything, and she had arranged to eat here at this modest place so Michele wouldn't have to stray far from her office.

Michele was the one who'd asked Ally a question she hadn't quite heard. The woman's brown eyes were curious under the thick, fashionable frames of her glasses, her face full, even cherubic, with perpetually pink cheeks.

An angel, Ally thought. Her adoption angel.

But, then again, everything seemed to have an aura about it today. She smiled as they waited for Cheryl to arrive.

Shaking off the effects of Jeremiah, Ally said, "Sorry, I didn't hear what you said."

"I was just asking how you're feeling." Michele took the linen napkin from the table and spread it over her lap.

"Oh, I'm doing well." *Too* well, Ally thought as she followed Michele's example with the napkin.

"It's always a little stressful being with the birth

mother, no matter how often you see her or how much she adores you."

"Adores me?"

"Ally." Michele clucked her tongue. "She *chose* you, and it wasn't just because of how cleverly you put together your portfolio, with all those artistic touches, or how she thought you'd provide a great life for the child. You have an appreciation of the simple things, and she was drawn to that. She keeps telling me that you're 'awesome but humble,' a wonderful combination."

"She kept mentioning those portfolio pictures of the horses and the country at our last meeting."

"Different things speak to different people. And she admires all the charitable work you've done. Good marks all around."

Ally was glad Michele was here, whether or not this was one of the official meetings they were required to have, because a neutral party eased the awkwardness between two strangers who were taking part in an emotion-laden transaction.

Ally hated using that word, *transaction,* but that's what this was, with an adoption agreement and everything. But it was an open adoption, where there would be the occasional picnic or event that allowed both Cheryl and Ally to spend time with the baby. Ally was even going to suggest that she could send pictures of the child to Cheryl if she wanted, although Ally wasn't sure she would, what with the way Cheryl had already confessed to never wanting a baby in the future. Still, it left room for the child to get to know Cheryl, and that was Ally's main concern.

It just seemed as if she had already made her peace with her decision to give up her baby, though.

When Cheryl came out of the doorway of the brick cottage that housed the café, she waved at Ally and Michele. She had corn-blond hair, big blue eyes and the cheekbones of a model; she even wore her rounded belly with aplomb, under a chic olive linen shorts suit. Once, Michele had commented that Ally and Cheryl had such similar coloring that the baby might even end up resembling Ally.

She hugged Cheryl then helped her to sit in a comfortable wicker chair and sat back down herself. They already had water, and Cheryl took a few gulps before setting the glass on the table, where patterns from the slatted overhead awning created shadows.

"Sorry I'm late," she said. "There was an accident on the 101."

"Not to worry," Ally said.

Cheryl leaned back in her chair, resting her hands on the armrests, her belly so big that Ally wanted to cup it, to feel the child under all that roundness.

"My brother was driving me, and he reminded me that it's nice to slow down every once in a while," Cheryl said. "Life has gone pretty fast these past couple of years. I've barely hauled in a breath since I started college, and now it seems like this adoption is flying by, too."

She'd taken the semester off to have the baby while staying at her brother's home, but Cheryl was the type who would be right back at the books after this. At least, that's how it seemed to Ally.

Would the girl ever slow down again, looking up

from her studies long enough to regret her decision to give up the baby?

A zing of fear flew through Ally. She wouldn't be able to bear it if Cheryl changed her mind about the adoption—and the closer they got to the due date, the more she worried about it.

"Things *are* going fast," Ally said. "But I don't mind that a bit."

Michele handed Cheryl a menu. "Sometimes all the pieces fall into place, like they did with the two of you, and we can move fast. Actually, eighty percent of our agency's families do adopt within the first year, so we've got a good track record."

Cheryl gave a perfunctory scan to the food list, then decided what she wanted within a minute, even before Michele or Ally.

"It seems like *everything* is on fast-forward," Ally said. "Last night, my garbage disposal broke, and I've been so distracted that I didn't fully realize I needed to fix it until this morning."

Ally stopped herself right there. The only reason she hadn't cared about the darn garbage disposal while cleaning up from dinner last night was that she'd been in such a state from Jeremiah. Her brain had only caught up this morning, when Mrs. McCarter, who'd thankfully gone straight to bed after she'd left Ally and Jeremiah alone outside, had mentioned it.

Michele put down her own menu. "Prepare yourself, Ally. A lot of things are going to go by the wayside with a newborn."

Ally smiled with such verve that she knew she had to seem giddy.

A newborn. Her own little baby.

But when she glanced over at Cheryl, she found the girl looking at the menu again, as if she was reconsidering her choice.

Trying not to read anything into that, Ally stilled the rush of fear and told herself that everything was going to go like clockwork.

Everything would go just fine.

A couple of hours later, Ally parked her old BMW in a mini-mall lot. The lunch had gone well, without any more paranoid moments for Ally.

Able to breathe easier now, she headed toward the hardware store, the coastal air making for a mild day, a hint of sea breeze on the wind.

But then, strangely, she felt a tickle, a sensation she usually felt whenever...

She turned around to find a familiar green pickup truck with an equally familiar person resting one arm on the steering wheel as he leaned out the window and tipped his cowboy hat to her.

"Afternoon," Jeremiah said, grinning, as if he was thinking about kissing her again.

Her skin sparked with a million popping nerve endings, and Ally stopped walking. Was this a coincidence or...

No, he couldn't be following her around. Even Jeremiah Barron, who had more tenacity than she'd seen in anyone, wouldn't go there.

As if reading her thoughts, he said, "I'm not stalking you, Ally. I was on my way to the market here."

"Then you'll be on your way to the airport, right?" she asked hopefully.

But from somewhere else inside her—the part that wondered what it would be like to be a not-so-good-girl—there was a yearning for him *not* to be going anywhere.

"I'm sticking around the area for a bit, checking things out," he said. A reminder that he was and always would be the business shark with an eye for new properties. "I'm still at the Sea View Hotel. You should hear the waves at night. They're almost enough to lull me to sleep."

Almost enough. Was he telling her that their kiss had kept him awake, too?

He nodded toward the hardware store. "You on a fix-it mission?"

"My garbage disposal decided to give me trouble, so I thought I would see if they have any handyman services." She'd been so addled that she hadn't thought to go online to check it out herself before this afternoon. Besides, she needed to pick up some nails for the pictures she would be hanging in the nursery.

"It just so happens," Jeremiah said, "that I'm pretty handy."

I'm sure you are, Ally thought, especially in relation to last night, even though he hadn't taken the opportunity to get handy with her during that kiss.

In fact, he'd been pretty restrained. He was the one who'd ended things, and she couldn't figure out why.

Just thinking about his lips against hers flipped her tummy and made her want to sigh.

But, none of that. *No* sighing.

Before she could tell Jeremiah that she had the repairs under control, he'd pulled into a parking space and was out of the truck, cowboy boots, jeans and all.

As he walked toward the hardware store entrance, Ally said, "Really, I don't need—"

"It's no problem," he said. "And I'll be in and out of your place before you know it. I'm going to head back to the hotel, eat a bite, then go home. I promise."

She watched him go into the store. She *did* need the disposal fixed. And if he had plans to leave soon anyway….

She followed him into the store, which smelled faintly of rubber. After asking her some details about the disposal, Jeremiah seemed to know just what he needed. She didn't trail him though, preferring to fetch those nails instead.

He was ready within ten minutes, and she met him at the checkout, her credit card in hand.

Jeremiah had his out, too.

"Thanks, but that's not necessary," Ally said, unwilling to be more in debt to him than she already was, with this favor as well as the roses. "I've got this."

He backed off without a protest, but his grin told her that he was enjoying her spunk.

It was only when they walked out of the store with their purchases that Ally realized just how stressed out something small like a garbage disposal could make a person. Just knowing that it was going to be taken care of made her feel a bit lighter.

So much going on right now—more than she would admit.

As they walked side by side, her arm brushed his

and she inhaled, then made sure they had a few inches between them.

If Jeremiah noticed, he didn't remark on it, and that wasn't like him.

Then again, hadn't there been a change in him last night, when he'd ended the kiss before she could?

Good heavens, just how far would she have let it go if he hadn't stopped?

As they came to her car, she used her remote to unlock it. It whimpered, just as she'd done at some point during that kiss. She didn't recall when—just that it had happened.

What was wrong with her?

He opened her door and she slid inside, but before he shut it, he braced his arms on the top of the car, his body blocking the door, making her feel cornered.

Weirdly, it was in a place she kind of liked.

"See you there, then," he said.

She held her breath, running her gaze over his wide chest, his flat stomach....

It took all the strength she had to stop, look ahead and start the engine.

He retreated, shutting the door at the same time, then watched her back out of her space and drive away.

This was a mistake, she thought. She shouldn't let him come back yet again, even to fix a garbage disposal. Why hadn't she just told him she could handle it herself?

Heart thumping all the way home, she finally made it up her driveway, Jeremiah's truck not far behind.

There was a car she didn't recognize in the driveway. As she got out, Jeremiah didn't ask about it—not until

Mrs. McCarter came out of the house, accompanied by the last person Ally expected to see here so soon.

"Ally cat!" Aunt Jess said, her arms open as she ran over for a hug, her long sun-kissed brunette hair flying behind her.

Laughing, Ally couldn't have been happier...until Jess ended the embrace and glanced at Jeremiah, who stood nearby greeting a delighted Mrs. McCarter.

From the expression on Jess's face, Ally knew she had a lot of explaining to do, both to Jess...

And to herself.

Chapter Seven

Jess led Ally into the house, down the long hall and into the first guest bedroom they came to.

She closed the door behind them. "You could have knocked me over with a feather. What is *he* doing here?"

Ally was pretty sure that saying she'd been asking herself the same thing wouldn't go over too well.

"He's fixing the garbage disposal," she said honestly, wishing she could just leave it at that.

Jeremiah was probably even now following Mrs. Mc-Carter into the garage, where Ally kept her supply of tools.

"The garbage disposal," Jess repeated, planting her hands on her skirted hips. "Is that all you've got to say when you have the biggest scoundrel in all of Texas here at your house?"

Ally lifted her hands, shrugging.

Naturally, that wasn't enough for Jess. "Ally, I saw all those roses he planted. And Mrs. McCarter told me about how Jeremiah Barron has been buzzing around you like a bee with a stinger ready to—"

"Jess, it's not that way."

"Then tell me, what way *is* it?"

What could she say?

He kissed me, and I can't stop thinking about it. Or, *You should see him when he's not at parties or around the regular crowds. He's different. He's...*

Well, she didn't know for certain what he was. But, more and more, she wanted to find out, in spite of every logical bone in her body.

Ally sat on the king-size bed, holding on to the brass bedpost. "All right, here's the truth. I'm not sure what's going on, Jess. But I've started to like having him around."

"I hate to say this, but the man makes his way through life manipulating people, and you know that as well as I do because you've spent half *your* life sticking to your guns and seeing right through people like him. Yet here you are, entertaining him, telling me that he's so very different than what you expected. Don't you think other women have thought the same darn thing about him, Al?"

Ally wanted to argue, wanted to tell Jess that she'd gotten a more thorough view into Jeremiah. That he was misunderstood by the world at large.

But *had* she just been spellbound by a master and was that the gist of it?

Yet, that notion didn't make sense. She had been so very good at ferreting out the liars from the rest during her time in high society—why hadn't some other smooth-talking cad blinded her?

Jess leaned back against the door. "I want to smack myself for telling Jeremiah where you went after the Howards' charity auction. I thought by letting him know that you'd taken off without saying goodbye to him, he would get the hint and leave you alone. You made it a point to shine him off, but that only seemed to spur him on, not dissuade him."

"And nobody leaves Jeremiah Barron in the dust," Ally whispered.

What was the truth and what was a lie when it came to him? Why did she even *care?*

She rested her head against the bedpost. "He really has been helpful, Jess, seeing to things around the house that don't seem so important in light of all that's going on with the adoption."

"Oh, so you just need a handyman. That's easy enough to take care of. Where are your yellow pages?"

"Stop kidding."

"No joke, Al."

Jess, of all people, was making it sound as if Ally just needed a man who could take care of her. And she hated the sound of that. For a while, she'd done just fine on her own, surrounding herself with the people she loved, like Mrs. McCarter and Jess—not people she'd hand chosen because they were "useful."

It was just that whenever Jeremiah was with her, he brought something to her life that Mrs. McCarter or Jess didn't bring.

But whatever that was, she would need to do without it. She would *have* to as a single mother, because

Jeremiah had told her once before that, in spite of whatever soft spots she thought he might be hiding within him, he wasn't the kind to settle down.

She didn't need fantasies of a husband figure to carry her through, even though it occasionally felt lonely thinking about how she really was on her own.

A single mom. She was going to have a *baby,* and even with her well-meaning company, she would be only one parent, not two.

Jess was measuring her with a frown, but Ally didn't want her to worry.

"He'll be gone soon, anyway," she said. "Back to Texas. Back to everything he was doing before he decided to come out here."

Her aunt lifted an eyebrow. "I'm not sure you can dismiss Jeremiah that easily. The man's been riding on his ego for years. His pride might be at stake."

Her aunt's words rang through the room. No one but Ally had seen that exposed moment at the charity auction when she'd caught Jeremiah cavorting with those kids, just before he'd tried to cover up his gentler side by brushing off her questions about having a family someday.

No one had seen him walk away after that kiss last night, turning back to her as if he'd wanted to make sure the moment had actually happened.

Ally got up from the bed. "You won't have to deal with him while you stay here since he's in a hotel by the beach, far enough away from us."

"That's good to hear." Jess moved out of the way as Ally went for the door. "Based on his reputation, I wouldn't have put it past him to pitch a tent on your lawn and inch his way closer to staying inside the house with every passing hour."

Ally laughed and shook her head, opening the door.

"Just…" her aunt began to say.

Ally paused, waiting for the rest.

Jess wrinkled her brow, then finished. "Never mind. You're smart and aware of what's what. I shouldn't fret about this."

"Then don't."

Ally moved into the hallway and walked toward the main part of the house, where Jeremiah would've come in from the garage by now.

Jess was right about one thing—he'd already found a way into her home.

And maybe even more.

"Someday, the baby's going to love this," Mrs. McCarter said, leaning on her cane in the Southwest-themed living room as Jeremiah finished setting up the high-powered telescope he'd purchased just this morning. Nearby, a large fish tank hummed, filled with broken wagon wheels and a crumbling adobelike home for the freshwater fish to swim through.

Even though he had work in the kitchen to get done, he'd started on this telescope first. Truthfully, he had quite a few gifts he'd bought this morning for Ally's child that he'd wanted to take out of the pickup and into the house before hunkering down with the garbage disposal. He'd actually planned on hiring someone to deliver the presents, but when he'd seen Ally at that mini-mall, it'd been as if fate had decided to wink at him, and he'd changed his mind about staying away from her.

Hell, frankly, he would've seized any chance to see Ally again. He craved it, especially since all he could think about was kissing her, holding her.

But he'd gotten all he was going to get, most likely. A kiss in a garden. And after today, he'd tip his hat to her and go.

Unless...

Jeremiah brushed off the thought. She wasn't going to ask him to stay, even if he wanted to hear it from a woman like her.

He aimed the telescope toward the window, peering through it, then stepped out of the way for Mrs. McCarter to do the same.

"I know the baby won't be able to use this for years," he said, "but I saw it and thought, what the hell."

Bull. He'd caught a glimpse of it in a store window and thought of Ally, impulsively snatching it right up, wondering if the gift would always serve to remind her of him and the night they'd talked about the stars.

The kind of night no other woman could have ever claimed to share with Jeremiah Barron.

He wasn't sure why it was important to have her remember him that way, but he liked the possibility of it. Liked it a lot.

Mrs. McCarter squinted through the eyepiece. "You bought enough for that baby to guarantee a gift per year, Jeremiah. Toys, outfits, even a supply of diapers to be delivered each week."

He didn't say anything about how practical Ally would want those kinds of things before any fancier gifts. In spite of her financial fall, she wasn't nearly destitute.

"They say a mother can never have enough of those. But what do I know?"

Mrs. McCarter looked up from the telescope. "I'd say you know quite a bit. You just don't care for anyone to realize it."

As the astute old woman grinned at him, Jeremiah nearly flushed. He'd been called out.

"I'll tell you something else, too," Mrs. McCarter said. "Ally doesn't make a show of it, but she can use all the support she can get right now, even if it's from a business associate who dabbles in home appliances and gardening."

The way Mrs. McCarter said "business associate" made him think that she hadn't bought into the supposed reason for his traveling out here. She'd probably known he was full of it before *he'd* even admitted it.

"Ally's got a tough road ahead of her," Jeremiah said. "She's taken on a lot, adopting as a single mom."

"And right now, I can tell you that her aunt Jess isn't exactly helping matters. Jess means well, but she strongly believes in a two-parent family. Ally doesn't need any more doubts about what she's doing." Mrs. McCarter went back to the telescope. "Don't get me wrong—when all's said and done, Jess will be behind Ally one hundred percent. She just needs to come to terms with Ally's decision and trust that Ally is going to be a fabulous mother, with or without a husband."

Husband.

A possessive surge overwhelmed Jeremiah, making him bristle. He didn't want to think of Ally being with another man, even though she would no doubt find one someday.

While he tried to make sense of the chaos whirling in him, Mrs. McCarter continued.

"Jess was raised by a single mom, and she wishes she'd had a father in the house, too. She missed a sense of stability, but I don't think that can be pinned on merely the lack of a dad. Not entirely. Her mother wasn't there much, either. Jess felt very alone when she was growing up, and she believes that if she'd had a father everything would've been wonderful. That's why Jess thinks Ally should have a husband—because she doesn't want the baby to ever feel as if he or she has been slighted."

Mrs. McCarter must've heard someone coming, because she stopped talking and began playing around with the telescope again.

Ally entered from the long hallway, and the sight of her—the straight, light hair, the heart-stopping shape of her delicate face, the vividness of her gaze—rocked Jeremiah.

He could look at her forever.

But he wasn't meant for forever. Hell, he wasn't even meant to go beyond a night or two.

"What's this?" Ally asked, gesturing toward the telescope, smiling with curiosity.

He barely even paid attention as Mrs. McCarter explained his shopping spree.

As Ally listened to her, Jeremiah wanted to damn everyone and everything and go to her, scoop her into his arms, bend her into another kiss…then more….

When Jessica entered the room, coming to sit on a desert-patterned couch, he dropped the fantasies. That strange protective streak lit him up again. "Afternoon, Jessica," he said.

"Hi, Jeremiah."

"You here to change some diapers?"

"Sure," she said. "Bring them on."

She laughed, but he noticed that Ally's smile was only halfhearted as she ran her hand over the toys that Mrs. McCarter had pulled out of their bags earlier and strewn over the hardwood floor, fussing over Jeremiah's kindness.

He spoke to Jessica again. "This is going to be a hard row to hoe, keeping up with a newborn."

"We'll be ready."

Time to get to the point. "Ally's got the heart of a lion, taking on the responsibility."

"Yes, she's very brave." Jessica smiled at him, but it was noncommittal, as cool as Ally's could sometimes be.

Did she want to add something else to the *brave* part? Did she want to say it was foolish for Ally to adopt on her own? Or was she just patronizing Jeremiah with her civil conversation?

Hell, if he could fix one more thing around this house before he left, this would be it—Aunt Jessica's attitude. He didn't know if he had any kind of shot at it, but why not give it the all-American try?

"It's nice to see someone who's willing to put a child first above everything else," he added, only now thinking about his dad and how he had seen fit to put *himself* first and all the rest of them a distant last.

Everyone was watching Jeremiah by now, but he

hardly cared. Ally was even looking at him with a sympathetic question in her eyes.

"To have someone in your life who loves you," he said, "someone who makes sacrifices without asking for anything in return... If a child has that in even one parent, he's lucky."

He didn't explain exactly what he suspected *his* mother had done to preserve the stability of the Barron household. Had she pretended she hadn't known anything about her husband's wandering libido, just to keep the peace in the family? Just to make her sons think that theirs was a stable and happy home?

Jessica was inspecting him as if she was weighing his reputation against what he'd just said. As if she was reconciling both in her mind.

Or maybe she was just thinking about Ally.

Either way, Jessica ended up keeping her tongue, just staring at the stuffed animals on the floor as Ally stood among them.

Several moments of silence beat past, ending only when Mrs. McCarter came over to pat Jeremiah on the back, as if she approved of him sticking his nose into Ally's business when, maybe, he shouldn't have. Then she used her cane to start walking.

"Let's get you unpacked, Jess," she said.

An invitation to scoot couldn't have been any clearer, and Jessica gave Jeremiah a polite parting glance, following the older woman.

But Ally didn't go anywhere. She stayed behind, hugging a stuffed elephant to her chest.

"Sorry if I overstepped," Jeremiah said, just now realizing how much tension he'd introduced to the room. He hadn't exactly meant to.

"No, I'm glad you said all that. I…I think I needed to hear it from someone other than Mrs. McCarter. Not that I don't take her opinions to heart, but there are times when hearing it *again* makes me that much more confident in what I'm doing."

Jeremiah hesitated, not wanting to start work on the garbage disposal just yet. But, second by second, he realized that maybe Ally wanted to be alone with the toys and stuffed animals…and even her thoughts.

He took a step toward the kitchen, but it was a tough step, because when he finished this one last task it would be time for him to leave.

He would have run out of reasons to be here.

Ally put a halt to his progress. "You said something about sacrifices, just like you knew someone—a parent—who'd made them for you, Jeremiah. Were you talking about your mom?"

Yup, she had read him like a dime-store novel. "Mom never said anything to me or Ty, but she had to know what my dad was doing behind her back with Aunt Laura. I don't know how they could've hidden it from her. She wasn't a woman who missed details."

"So she stayed with your father, even if she was being cheated on, and it was for the sake of you and your brother."

"I don't know for sure, but in my heart, I feel like it went down that way."

His heart. He'd just confessed to having one, and it clearly hadn't escaped Ally, either. She was looking at him as if he would never be able to hoodwink her or cover up anything about himself again.

He couldn't stop himself from adding, "I wouldn't trade my mother for anyone, Ally, and your baby is going to feel the same way about you."

When she smiled at him in gratitude, her gaze going misty, he felt beaten to a pulp.

Totally conquered.

A dull, painful throb overcame him. He longed to say everything he was feeling—every crazy, messed up, nonsensical sweet something that was confusing the hell out of him.

But, out of self-preservation and habit, he tried to cover himself instead. Tried hard.

Ally sighed, as if she hoped he would offer more to her. When he didn't, she said, "I wish it was already dark out. I'd like nothing more than to take that telescope outside and just look at the stars and have a few minutes when I'm not stressing out about a broken appliance or getting the nursery in shape. I also don't want to think about whether my child is going to be angry at me for denying him or her a father one day."

"Maybe you just need to get out of the house, period," he said impulsively.

He definitely had her full attention now.

Courage pumped through him. Hope.

"Maybe you need a ride," he added. "Just a little time on the open road where you don't have to worry about a thing."

She clutched that stuffed elephant as if she was holding on to her perceptions of Jeremiah Barron, the silver-tongued devil.

Was she wondering what he intended to do on a ride, just like the one he'd taken her on back at the Howards' ranch in that Jeep?

As he was about to tell her to forget about it, she put down the elephant.

"Actually, I'd love a break," she said. "Let's go."

Then she made her way toward the patio doors, leaving Jeremiah tongue-tied and twisted.

Ally had no idea what she was doing, but she liked doing it.

With the pickup's window open, the wind bathed her face, sending her hair flying free as they drove down an isolated stretch of country road, past green hills that rose and fell with the grace of waves.

She'd just wanted to get away, not only from Jess and her judgments about Jeremiah and the adoption, but from the stress of making sure everything around the house was perfect for the baby.

When they neared a sign that read Tarot Vineyards she pointed to it.

"Turn here?"

If Jeremiah was surprised at her suggestion, he didn't show it, and he took the graveled side road.

She'd been to this small winery before, when she'd bought the house, and it was as peaceful as it got, with an ivy-covered brick cottage, bird fountains and a pathway that led toward a copse of trees.

Sneaking a glance at Jeremiah, she tried not to tell herself that she'd suggested this detour because she wanted to be alone with him.

She watched how he drove with a casual grace, one

arm draped on the windowsill, the air playing with his hair. Being with him reminded her of the day he'd made off with her in that Jeep on the Howards' ranch.

It was just that, this time, Ally had come willingly.

After he parked the pickup in a tiny lot, he came around to open her door for her while putting on his hat. Then he offered a hand.

"I've got to get ahold of you before you slide over to the driver's seat and take off with my ride," he said.

He was remembering, too.

But this time, she accepted his hand.

At the skin-to-skin contact, she sizzled. A shocking jolt of yearning fired her up, too, and she hoped he couldn't hear her blood roaring through her veins.

He folded his fingers over hers, enveloping her in warmth. The gesture was simple but so erotic that it turned her all the way into flame.

Dumb. This was the dumbest thing she could've possibly done, taking off by herself with Jeremiah.

But why *not* do it?

Why shouldn't she take a harmless ride with him just one time before they went on with their lives?

He helped her alight from the truck and, when she hit the ground, she removed her grip from his faster than she meant to.

He paused, as if she'd slighted him, but then he shut the door, walking toward the little cottage. Next to it, stone fountains splashed among pine lawn furniture and benches.

"I drove by this place on one of my ride-arounds," he said.

"While you were looking at property?"

"Believe it or not, Ally, I did actually get some work done while I've been here."

Well, listen to him—reminding her that he had a life besides the one where he spent all his time chasing around women. Point taken.

He held open the cottage door for her, and they went inside. Wine bottles lined the shelves, and a young male college student sat at the bar, a postgrad physics book open in front of him.

They ordered two glasses of pinot noir, then took them out to the seating area.

When Jeremiah sat on a love seat, she took a spot next to him without really thinking about it...until she realized that there was maybe a foot of space between them.

She ignored it, even though the area seemed to shiver with voltage-charged anticipation.

"What did Mrs. McCarter say when you called to tell her where you'd gone?" Jeremiah asked, resting one booted ankle over his knee.

"Nothing much. She knows there's some tension between me and Jess. But I said you and I were going to the market, not to a winery. I'll just tell her that we had a change of plans when I show up with a new case of pinot—something she'll highly appreciate."

"So Mrs. McCarter likes her grapes?"

"Very much. I think that's part of the reason why, when I asked her to come out to my place, she jumped at the chance. This region around San Luis Obispo exploded with wineries over the last couple of decades. Mrs. McCarter and Jess were even planning on renting a limo one day before the baby is born so they can hit the tastings, but they'll have to do it soon since Cheryl's due date is coming up fast."

A moment passed. Thinking about Cheryl and the baby stressed her out, so she changed the subject.

"Thanks again for sticking up for me with Jess." She'd guessed that Mrs. McCarter might've said something to him about the situation and he'd taken it upon himself to speak in Ally's favor.

"You already thanked me."

"I know, but it was…" She stopped herself short of saying, "sweet."

Yet there was no pulling the wool over his eyes.

"It was sweet of me?" he asked, grinning.

She nodded, and he laughed.

"That's something I don't hear often. 'Sweet.'"

Once again, awareness descended like a mist that breathed over Ally's skin, and she realized that neither of them had even taken a sip of their wine yet.

She raised her glass, tasting the full body of the pinot noir—the hint of cranberry, pepper, earthiness.

He did the same but didn't drink any more than that. "I thought I should return the kindnesses you've shown me, Ally. That's all I was doing."

"Kindnesses?" *Really?* "Jeremiah, I've done nothing but try to kick you out of sight since you've gotten here."

"Have you? I didn't notice."

When he laughed again, it was low and deep, and it didn't take any more wine for a sliding trickle of weakness to travel down the length of Ally.

"Seriously though," he said, "you've shown me a thing or two while I've been here. It's been good for me to see that even though a person can get into a situation that makes them *feel* alone, a person doesn't necessarily have to *be* alone."

"What do you mean by that?"

He glanced at her as if she should already know. "Don't tell me you haven't felt like you've pretty much been on your own with this whole adoption thing, especially with the way Jess feels about it. She's the only true blood family you have left, right? You might've hoped that her support would be easier to get."

"Yes."

"That can't feel good. But watching you rise above it all has just shown me... Well, that I can rise above it, too."

"With your family?"

He still didn't drink, just sat there, hardly joking around or laughing now.

Was this the real Jeremiah?

Or was this the man with the silver tongue, manipulating Ally with emotion just to get what he wanted in the end?

He knew how to operate around women, and he could've used heart-to-heart scenarios like this a hundred times before, but Ally wouldn't believe it. She had seen that naked flicker in his gaze—the split in his armor—too many times to think it wasn't genuine.

True belief wrapped around her. She would bet her reputation on the fact that he was being real.

"I guess," he finally said, "that being around you has made me think that I can have the strength to put my own family together."

She rested her hand over his.

He wound his fingers through hers, but she knew deep inside that it wasn't because he wanted to seduce her—it was because he needed to hold to someone or something else just as much as everyone did.

And that was when Ally knew she was losing her heart to Jeremiah Barron.

Chapter Eight

Jeremiah wasn't used to sitting around while just holding a woman's hand. This sort of quiet gesture wasn't even in his repertoire unless he was leading a lady to a shadowed place where they could be alone together: a nook, a balcony, a bedroom.

But as Ally kept contact with him—innocently, without expectation—he found that he was actually partial to hand-holding.

This was what it was like to really be with a woman when you weren't planning on getting something from her. This was what Tyler had found with his new wife, Zoe—a sense of rightness, as if there wasn't anyone but her in your world. It even made Jeremiah think that maybe Ally was the one person who wouldn't believe he was weak for feeling the way he did around his family... or her.

Most importantly, it was also as if she wouldn't even

have to say another word for him to have faith that there might be hope for him in the days ahead.

Something about Ally—her own strength and determination in life—showed him that hope wasn't a false notion and, around her, he didn't mind entertaining it.

But then he started to wonder… Was *she* just as moved by such a simple gesture?

When she glanced down at their joined hands, he thought that maybe she was, because she inhaled deeply before letting go of him.

He flexed his hand, wanting to have the last few seconds back. But she'd obviously broken a rule within herself and was backing off. Maybe she was even afraid of what would happen now, since she'd indicated that she wasn't as closed off to him as she'd tried to make him think during these past couple of days.

That got to Jeremiah. Whether he would cop to it or not, he'd been trying to show her that he wasn't what everyone thought he was.

He'd been letting his true self slip out hint by hint, just to see if she would give him a sign that she might accept him.

Had he just gotten that sign with the way she'd touched him?

As she put her wineglass on the low wood table in front of them, he did the same.

Damn it, he truly did miss the feel of her hand in his. But maybe she'd really only been comforting him, like the softhearted philanthropist she was.

Yet, when he noticed the raging blush on her cheeks, he knew it couldn't have been as uncomplicated as that. There had to be more, and the protective streak in Jeremiah reared up again, as if he wanted to defend her against even himself. It disgusted him that he'd set out to play what amounted to seductive poker with her in the first place.

What would everyone say if they could see him now? Jeremiah Barron, slayed by the purest of touches?

She motioned toward his full glass of wine. "You done?"

"Yup. I like it. But I only needed a taste to know that."

Did she sense an innuendo there—something to do with how she'd only needed to hold his hand for him to know that he wanted much more?

He hadn't meant it that way.

But then she did something that made him think that he didn't know what was running through her mind at all.

She stood and pointed toward a path that wound into a gathering of trees.

"There's this great part of the winery that no one really sees. Let's explore for a bit, then we'll go into the cottage and grab some stock before we go."

They took the path, and it wasn't long until they came upon a patch of trees where flowers had been planted near the roots. Some of the mini-gardens had dolls, framed pictures of crayon drawings presenting the sky or cities like Paris. Nearby, just off the path, a cute little shack stood, its doors open so that a splash of more flowers peeked out.

"The first time I came to this winery," she said, standing near a thrust of pink flowers accompanied by several pictures of race cars, "they told me that the Tarot family started this tradition. They wanted to plant the seeds for their futures. Their friends started doing it, too, and soon more people decided to join in." She smiled. "After the baby's birth, I'm getting a space here, as well."

She was absolutely beaming, and Jeremiah felt the same bloom of light inside of him. But the glow was deceptive, because he couldn't imagine his own family ever taking part in something like this.

Then again, what had he just told Ally?

Being around you has made me think that I can have the strength to put my own family together.

He hadn't just been talking about reconciling with his father, either. Jeremiah had actually been thinking of *his* future, and if it could possibly have his very own family in it.

The thought hadn't even scared him. In fact, Jeremiah had felt a sense of purpose for the very first time in his life, as if he might just have a reason to leave work each weekday night. As if there would finally be something... someone...to come home to.

Ally caught the look on his face, and he couldn't guess what she might've seen there. The same kind of yearning he'd noticed in her when she'd been watching those kids at the Howards' ranch?

"Here I am prattling on about baby stuff again," she said.

"No, I like hearing your plans." He stuffed the tips of his fingers into his jeans pockets, not knowing what else to do with himself.

"You don't mind how I go on and on about it?" she asked.

"I surely don't. It's good to see someone who's so

unabashedly happy about the direction her life's going. It's refreshing."

"You say that as if you think you won't ever be happy again yourself."

Had he *ever* been?

Certainly there had been a few moments in his history when he'd been honestly happy. But the only ones he could remember right now, as he stood next to Ally, were the ones that involved her.

Seeing her across the room at that Red Cross charity event and deciding that she was the one he wanted that night… Kissing her as the rain tapped on the window behind them in the Howards' mansion… Taking part in her joy every time she even thought about that baby…

"I just never knew," he said, "that happiness took so much work."

"You think it does?"

"Hell, yeah. In a perfect world, welcoming a new person into the family, just like you're about to do, would be an occasion to celebrate. Then there's my world." He glanced at the flowers near the toe of one boot. "Chet's a good guy, and any family would be glad to have him, but that's not how it shaped up to be with us."

"I made the choice of bringing someone else into the fold. You didn't."

He'd never been able to talk to anyone like this—not even his brother Ty. Sure, they could be blunt with each other, but there'd always been a wall of shame between them, as if they'd both been trying to stay strong while the scandal had battered away at their foundations.

Ally was good at listening. And, for some reason, she even sounded…invested.

Jeremiah took his hands out of his pockets. He was so tired of playing games around her. He only wanted something real, like this conversation.

Like her.

Letting down another layer of defense, he said, "Here's the thing with Chet…. It's no big secret that I'm not the number one son in the Barron crowd. And, when Chet came down to Texas, I expected him to be put right in the same place I was—outside of the golden orbit my brother Ty casts. But my father took my brand spanking new brother right in."

"He *was* given a copresidency with you and Tyler right off the bat."

Jeremiah nodded.

Ally's tone was conciliatory. "It had to hurt when Chet was given something so important like that without even earning it."

She seemed to know that Jeremiah had spent a lifetime trying to be worthy of every bit and crumb his father had parsed out to him.

Was she the only person who could see that in him?

He moved on to the next little garden, this one decorated with pictures of a family—one of those studio deals where everyone was posed and smiling in their Sunday best. There were yellow flowers, pinwheels and rocket ships in this plot, and Jeremiah remembered long ago when he'd dreamed of flying to the stars one day, too.

"The reason Chet got that copresidency," Jeremiah said, giving her more of the story than he ever had, "was because my uncle Abe had talked my father into it. Abe had already been diagnosed with cancer, and he wanted to give Chet an incentive to stay since they were on the outs. Abe didn't have to go so far though. Chet would've stuck around through thick and thin. But that's just how my family works—through machinations, in business and...otherwise."

Ally came up behind him. He could feel her on his skin.

"What do you mean by 'otherwise'?" she asked. "Are you talking about personal relationships, too?"

Normally, he would've found a way out of an explanation that cut so deep. He might have used a charming turn of phrase, or maybe an excuse to attend to some business on the other side of a room.

But when he turned and saw Ally's beautiful seascape eyes, every last piece of him broke apart, drifting toward her.

"Jeremiah," she said. "Just what makes you act the way you do with women?"

Her bluntness sliced even deeper. "Why do you want to know?"

"Why wouldn't I?"

She never took her gaze off of him. Her curiosity enflamed him, licked heat through every inch of his body.

Could he hope that she was asking because she'd gotten past his reputation?

In the past, this was where the playboy's escape machine would've been roaring to life so he wouldn't have to deal with telling truths. But around Ally, that's not who he was.

He was somehow more, and he wanted to live up to that with her.

"Are you asking if there was some girl who shattered my heart and started me off on my wanton path years ago?" he asked.

"We all have experiences that shape us."

"And for you it was Marco."

"That's right."

He couldn't do any less than return the candidness.

"Then I guess we could talk about the dark ages, when there *was* a girl. Nancy."

"How long ago?"

"College."

Ally tilted her head, as if she was wondering about this girl. "There's no one who's broken your heart since then?"

Just you, he thought randomly.

But she'd done no such thing.

Not yet, anyway.

He was more of an enigma than ever, and she wanted to solve him.

Wanted *more* from him, because she knew answers were there, and it would snap her heart in two to learn that she'd been wrong about him.

"There haven't been any more heartbreakers after Nancy," he said. But he uttered it in a flat tone, as if he wasn't about to put himself out there far enough to risk getting hurt.

Ally would've bet her last dollar that he did care, though.

"What was she like?" Ally asked.

"You mean, who was this girl who got Casanova to walk the line for a short time?" He shuffled a boot. "She wanted to be a teacher. Little kids, grade school, maybe even kindergarten." He slid Ally a glance. "She liked children a lot, too."

From the way he looked at her, warmth flared in Ally's core. It was as if he admired her nurturing spirit. As if he was drawn to it.

When a bird called from a nearby tree, he glanced up in its direction. "Yeah, I came dangerously close to having dreams of settling down with Nancy. I actually thought she was meant for me, if you can believe that."

"I can. I used to feel that way about Marco, too, until I learned that he didn't want the family life that I did."

"But you weren't willing to change for him. I was willing to do it for Nancy, though. I would've done it in a blink if I could've managed it."

At his wistful tone, Ally just stood there, uncomprehending for a second. There was real regret in his voice, although with the way he was studiously watching the treetops, as if to find that calling bird, she would've bet that he would give anything to hide the vulnerability.

"What happened with her?" she asked.

He narrowed his eyes. "After I did my damnedest to be a one-woman man and utterly failed, she decided that we wouldn't work out."

"You cheated on her?"

His jaw clenched, and he didn't have to say anything else.

A heaviness took over Ally. But surely he'd changed since those years. It'd been a long time ago.

He spoke again. "After that, every time I even glanced at another girl—no matter how harmlessly—Nancy said that I made her wonder if I was just going to cheat again. It was too much for a relationship to handle in the end."

"Would you have stayed faithful to her, though? If she'd stayed with you?"

"I wanted to—with all I had." He shook his head. "But she unloaded me but good and, in hindsight, if I were her I probably would've done the same, because I wouldn't have expected much more out of me, either."

"If I didn't know better, I'd say that's your dad talking, Jeremiah."

His gaze widened, and she knew she'd spoken too honestly.

"Sorry," she said. "I shouldn't have said that."

The bird stopped its calling, as if it sensed the taut air down below.

Jeremiah stared at the ground now. "It needed to be said. Here I am, partly in charge of one of the biggest corporations in the country, and I still get rankled by disapproval from the old man. But at least keeping him firmly in mind has done one thing for me—it's showed me that I don't want to end up like him, even though that's probably where I'm headed."

"No, you're not."

The force of her conviction made him look up, and the second their gazes connected, Ally withstood the zing of desire.

"Unless your father would follow a woman halfway across the country to plant roses," she said, "and buy her some much-appreciated baby stuff and fix up her house during a pretty stressful time for her, you're *nothing* like your dad. You only are if you didn't mean a bit of it."

She was offering him a challenge, but it wasn't really because *she* doubted him. She wondered if *he* doubted himself.

He didn't look away from her, and his eye contact reached deep, curling around her insides and flipping them over until she keened low and sharp.

"When I first came out here," he said, "I admit, it was because you ran away from me, and I couldn't stand for that. Nobody had done that to me before. But then…" He took off his hat, slowly lowering it. "Then I realized that, day by day, I wanted to come back to your place, and it wasn't just because I had the yen to play in a garden and fix a garbage disposal, or because of some Galveston property, either."

His words lured her, even as the old reasons whipped through her like ghosts she wanted to exorcise: his reputation. His willingness to do anything to get what he wanted in business and pleasure. Her determination to be the best example she could for a child.

But the longer they looked at each other, the more the gulf between them closed.

And closed.

Maybe she even took a step toward him. Or maybe he took one toward her.

All she knew was that she believed him when he said that his reasons for coming back to her had been stronger than either of them had admitted.

Before her brain could catch up, she was in his arms, clutching at the sleeves of his shirt.

She shouldn't do this….

But she was going to.

His mouth crushed down on hers and, at the first explosion of contact, she moaned, her eyes closing. A field of glittery stars blinded her, spangling downward until they got to her chest, lower, settling in her belly like needling points of light.

He slid a hand up to her hair, dug into it, bruising her mouth with the force of his kiss.

The electric light in her belly intensified as he bent her backward slightly, one of his hands supporting her in the small of her back. Then the zapping current flowed lower, between her legs, buzzing, making her want him more than she'd ever wanted a man before.

Somehow, they stumbled off the path, into the trees, toward that shack with the flowers in it.

When his tongue parted her lips, she welcomed him, stroking his every stroke, getting greedy as her hands bunched his shirt, pulling him closer.

How could she have ever denied herself this?

But another question formed in the haze of her mind—how could she live *without* this?

The rashness of the thought disappeared as they barged into the shack. He closed the door, and her knees buckled, the momentum lowering her to the ground.

He came with her. "Ally…"

Yet she wasn't letting him go, and she clutched his hair at the back of his head, bringing his mouth to hers again.

She wanted all of him, didn't care about what would happen afterward. It was a new thrill for her, letting go like this, seizing these last days before her life would change—when she wouldn't have time to see what it would be like to lose control for one hour, one day.

Letting her palms roam over his chest, she felt the muscle underneath, the fantasy of flesh and the hardness of male. Unstoppable, she yanked his shirt out of his jeans, wanting skin under her fingers.

She skimmed his ribs, his abs, and he sucked in a breath, then tightened his grip on her hair.

"Maybe this is enough," he said.

"No."

She didn't want to talk, just wanted his hands on her, and she grabbed one of them, leading it up to a breast. As she breathed against his mouth—warm, breath*less*—she felt as light as air.

He'd slowed their frantic pace, touching her as if he'd fantasized about it many times before. Ally had never thought of herself as a fantasy, and it thrust at her down deep, where she'd felt nearly empty for months and months.

"Look at you," he said, his voice gritty. "Just look at you."

He was tracing the center of a breast with his thumb, and it pebbled through her bra, her sundress. She couldn't help rising to her knees, glancing down, watching him. She'd never done that before—watched.

Marveled.

Been a little wicked.

When she pulled down the thick strap of her dress, revealing more of her lacy bra, he was the one who groaned this time.

And, just like the man who knew what he wanted,

he eased the material all the way from her breast, as if to get a stolen glance.

She still watched him, her pulse pounding between her legs. It only beat harder when he bent, touching his tongue to her nipple.

Biting her lip, she stifled an excited sound, but he heard it. She knew, because he took his time in tasting her breast again, one slow, lazy lick, as if he enjoyed knowing what it did to her.

She couldn't take it, and she pulled down her dress more, exposing her entire breast. He cupped it, and she leaned back her head, dying a little inside while he took her nipple into his mouth—warm, wet….

As he sipped, he sketched a hand to her thigh, stroking it.

The simultaneous caresses drove her mad, and agonized, she moved with him, hoping he'd move his hand up, to the apex of her thighs.

"Yes," she whispered, urging him on. "Oh, yes…"

Her voice seemed to strike something in him, and he stopped, just breathing against her skin, then wrapping both his arms around her, pulling her in for an embrace.

As he held her, Ally paused, embarrassed that he was the one putting a halt to things again.

Good girl?

Hardly.

Then a dark thought intruded on her. It must've been hiding out inside her someplace, back where she'd put it on the night they'd spent underneath the stars.

It must have come out when he'd been honest about

not being able to stop himself from being a good-time guy, even if he'd been committed to another woman.

That dark thought exploded into a question: What if he was putting a halt to their kisses now because everything *had* been a game for him and he was letting her know now that she'd already lost?

No, she shouldn't be thinking it....

As he slid his hands up, adjusting her bra and dress so that she was covered, then cupping her face, she saw the intensity in his gaze.

The certainty that this *wasn't* a game to him.

She tried to look away, but it was too late.

"You don't trust me," he said.

He thought that she believed he was never going to change. But she hadn't doubted it until he'd told her that story about college.

Just as she was about to explain, he kissed her once again, and she tasted a hint of resignation in it.

As his tenderness ripped at her, she tried to say something, but he only helped her to her feet.

"I've got to get you back before they think I made off with you," he said.

"Jeremiah..."

He opened the shack door, then went ahead to the path, where he'd dropped his cowboy hat without her even knowing it. She followed him, fumbling for words—an explanation of what he'd seen in her gaze.

He put that hat back on his head, covering himself, then waited for her.

Without much to say, they went back to his pickup. He helped her in, as always, and as he went around to the other side, she thought, *How am I ever going to make him see that I didn't think he was playing with me?*

Then her phone rang.

He was just getting into the cab when he heard it, too.

"Go ahead," he said.

"But…"

"It's fine. Go ahead."

She would just take a glimpse at the ID screen. Nothing could be as important as this….

But she was wrong.

She gasped, flipped open the phone, answered it. "Hello?"

Michele, her adoption facilitator, got right to the point. "Ally, Cheryl's in labor. It's time."

"It's…time?" Tears came to Ally's eyes.

She could feel Jeremiah watching her, as if he knew this was it. Her life was never going to be the same.

But hadn't that been her feeling during the kiss, too?

Jeremiah started up the engine. "Where're we going?"

"You don't have to—"

He turned to her, and there was such stalwart determination in his gaze that she didn't say anything more.

"Where, Ally?"

Her heart flew back to him again as she realized that, even after everything, the so-called fly-by-night guy wasn't going to leave her stranded.

Not even with a baby on the way.

Chapter Nine

Even before Ally had answered that phone, Jeremiah had known that it *was* time.

Time for him to leave her for good, if he was really going to do it.

How did he know? She'd gotten the same look in her eyes that he'd seen in his college girlfriend—that question, "How long will it be before you go back to the way you were?" It made his stomach sink.

Yeah, it was definitely time to go.

Nevertheless, here he was now, in Ally's private hospital room. Technically, the baby who was being given up by its birth mother was just as much the hospital's patient as Cheryl was, so that's why the child would have its own quarters. And Ally was there to take care of the newborn, staying with the baby, holding it, bonding like the new mother she was about to become.

He sat watching her pace the linoleum floor. He

would've been a complete creep to leave her in the lurch. But he would be out of here soon. And he meant it this time.

The adoption facilitator had already drawn up a birth plan and given it to the hospital, so the staff was basically treating Ally like one of their patients, checking her in to this room, bringing her food. The only inconvenience seemed to be that she couldn't be in the delivery room with the birth mother and the baby, and Jeremiah could see the wear and tear on Ally.

"What time is it?" she asked, stopping her pacing for a second.

Her hair was askew. It was the only time Jeremiah had ever seen it out of place, and he wasn't sure if it was because she'd been running her hands through it in her anxiety or…

His thoughts strayed back to what had gone on at that winery, where they'd kissed each other senseless, plus a little more.

It all came back with a pounding that wasn't so much physical as emotional. And that was another reason to get out of here—because he didn't know what to do with these feelings she brought out in him.

"It's now five minutes since you asked what time it was before," he said, injecting some levity into his tone, thinking they both needed it.

"And there's no news about the baby yet?" Ally nervously pushed back her hair. "Even on the phone, Michele said the baby was on his or her way and that the delivery was happening fast. The baby's due date isn't even here, and I was hoping their estimation wouldn't be that off…. The nursery's not even done yet…."

"The cradle's in your room, right?"

"Yes, but—"

"Ally, why don't you sit down until Michele gets back with an update?"

She shook her head, walking toward the door, which was open. Outside in the hallway, nurses passed by, carrying clipboards, going about their business.

When they'd checked Ally in, everyone had looked at Jeremiah as if he was going to be a father, just as she was going to be a mother, and he felt like an impostor, even though he was determined to stick by Ally's side.

For as long as she needed him.

But how long would that be? From this point on, she would have a baby, and he knew that he had no business hanging around with her any longer.

He glanced at his watch again, needing to occupy himself. Despite everything, Ally's anxiety was his own, because he wanted everything to go right, too.

"You said your house is at least an hour away?" The winery was much closer to the hospital, so he hadn't hesitated in taking her straight here, although he didn't know what more he could do for her. "Jessica and Mrs. McCarter should arrive soon."

They were the ones who belonged here—not him.

Ally stopped her pacing, sending him an unexpected, soft smile that just about tore out his heart. "*You're* here, though."

She said it as if she needed him...*wanted* him around.

And he realized that he didn't want to be anywhere else *but* here, even with that candid gaze she'd revealed to him at the winery.

"I've got nowhere better to go," he said.

Ally's smile grew. So did his heart.

But then a voice sounded in the hallway, and that snagged her attention back to the situation at hand.

When nobody came busting into her room with baby news, he said, "Don't worry. Everything's going fine in that delivery room. I'd put a bet on it."

"It's not just…that."

Her tone was ragged, and Jeremiah stood from his chair, his first instinct to comfort her.

He walked toward her. "What else is it?"

She twisted her dress, hesitating, then she shook her head, as if the words weren't coming easily.

"Ally?" he asked.

She looked up at him with shiny, tear-brimmed eyes. "Cheryl's in there giving birth to a child, and that has to do something to a mother. It has to bring out high emotions, and I'm scared to death that when she looks at that little baby…"

"Shhh."

Jeremiah held Ally against him, and she wrapped her arms around his waist, burying her face against his chest.

"What if she calls this whole thing off?" she asked.

"Don't think that way. Don't ruin this day by dwelling on something that won't happen."

"But Cheryl's going to be spending time alone with the baby. It's in the adoption agreement. She's allowed to say goodbye, and then the facilitator is going to ask her if this is what she really wants to do. She has an opportunity to take it all back. She can contest the adoption up to thirty days after the birth."

Thirty days of hell. Jeremiah hugged Ally tighter, wanting to shield her.

"And after those thirty days," he said, "you're going to have a happy life with your new child. You'll see, Ally. You'll see."

They stayed like that, in each other's arms, for what seemed like a lifetime. Jeremiah never wanted to let her go, and it didn't have anything to do with carnal impulses, either. He wanted to be here as long as it took for her to stop trembling.

He even wanted to see the look on her face when they brought that baby to her....

His shirt had gotten wet from her tears, and he stroked her hair.

"Jeremiah?" she finally whispered.

"Yeah."

She sniffed, angled her head so that she was looking at him.

His heart...

It wasn't his anymore. Maybe it hadn't been for a while.

"Remember what you said about how I make you think that a person doesn't have to be in a situation alone?" she asked. "You make me feel like I'm not going to be that way. It's good to have Mrs. McCarter, and even Aunt Jess, too.... But I don't know if anyone could've talked me down the way you just did."

There went that glow in him again. "You're not nervous now?"

"No, I'm still about to jump out of my skin." She

gave a little laugh that sounded as if it was on the edge of more tears. "But *you're* steady. And I'm glad circumstance brought you here to be with me now."

She went back to laying her head against his chest.

God. If she had found the purpose in her life with this baby, Jeremiah had just found his, too.

Her.

How long he would fit into this existence of hers, he just didn't know. It couldn't be forever though. Today had just been full of high emotion, and he was sure that as soon as it burned off and life settled into normal for Ally, she wouldn't need him around at all. She would go back to looking at him with distrust. He couldn't imagine it any other way.

As disappointment weighed him, he heard footsteps on the tile.

Ally lifted her head, and he turned around to find a brunette in glasses and a business skirt suit.

"Michele…?" Ally said, obviously hoping the woman had news.

She was smiling, her gaze tearful. "Hi, Mom. You've got a beautiful little baby girl."

Ally might've fallen to the floor in utter joy and relief if Jeremiah hadn't been there to prop her up. He'd even brought her to a cushioned chair, helping her to sit down with the utmost gentleness.

He stayed with her for the next twenty minutes or so as she shook, giving in to her tears.

But Ally didn't want her baby to see her as an emotional wreck, no matter whether her little girl would recognize that quality or not at this point in her new life.

Ally didn't want to give off the impression of a woman who was terribly afraid of losing the child she so dearly wanted.

What *had* Cheryl thought when she'd first seen the baby? Did she want to keep her?

As the thoughts chomped on Ally, Jeremiah made sure they both sanitized with gel. His skin was warm on hers as he rubbed it into her hands.

"A little girl," he said, his voice rough with emotion.

His reaction made her tear up even more.

Luckily, just after about twenty minutes, when she'd contained herself, Michele came back into the room alone.

"How's Cheryl?" Ally asked.

"Fine as can be, but she'd like to have a moment alone with her brother while we bring the baby in here. You can see Cheryl soon, if you'd like."

"I would."

Then Jeremiah took hold of Ally's hand as a nurse appeared in the doorway, and in her arms...

Ally choked back a sob. In her arms was a pink-swathed bundle, with a tiny pink face and a cap on her head.

"Are you ready?" Michele asked.

"Yes," Ally said. *Yes.*

Jeremiah let go of her hand, backing away. She felt his absence sharply, but he remained in the room as the nurse brought over her baby.

She eased the child into the cradle of Ally's arms. Her baby's eyes were closed, her lips pursed, sweeter than anything Ally had ever seen.

Tears spilled down her face, but they weren't worried or nervous tears. This was what she'd been meant to be—a mother.

"Hi, Caroline," Ally said, brushing her finger over the baby's oh-so-soft cheek. The child stirred in the blanket, her eyes still closed, her fists bunched. The most perfect baby ever.

And when Ally looked up, she found Jeremiah right there, smiling, with an emotional glint in his eyes she'd never seen…nor expected.

He was a real man, not just a playboy or a tycoon. And he was touched, maybe even overwhelmed, by seeing mother and daughter together.

She glanced back down at Caroline, thinking of their future: nights spent sitting in front of the fireplace while she hummed lullabies to her child. The smell of baby powder and soft skin. The feel of her baby held against her heart.

All of it was right there in her daughter's beautiful little face.

Time flew by because, suddenly, she had to give Caroline back to the nurse. Her arms felt awfully empty as she watched her baby go through the door.

Ally pressed her hand to her chest. It hurt.

But then Jeremiah was there again, his palm on her shoulder, making the anguish subside with every quickening beat of her pulse.

When they locked gazes, there was no need to say anything. He'd been here during the most important time of her life. He was the only one who would ever be able to share that with her.

The only one…

Michele cleared her throat from across the room. Ally couldn't even recall whether her facilitator had left and only returned now, or if she'd been here the entire time.

"They'll be bringing the baby back in about twenty, thirty minutes," Michele said. "Would you like to check in on Cheryl in the meantime? She should be ready for you."

Ally nodded, rising from the chair. She took a step forward but, on impulse, turned around and hugged Jeremiah, loving the feel of that strong chest, those capable arms.

Loving that he would be here when she got back.

He smiled at her as she left him in the room to wait for Jess and Mrs. McCarter to arrive, to catch them up on what was going on.

Please, God, Ally thought. *Please make it so that Cheryl didn't change her mind. Please...*

When she got to the birth mother's room, Ally could see that Cheryl was wiped out, her eyes reddened as she conjured a sad smile for Ally. The man who must've been her brother—he looked just like her with his blond hair and big blue eyes—greeted her, too.

Ally didn't even say anything to Cheryl, just took her hand in both of hers and pressed her cheek to it, unable to speak because her throat had completely closed off.

They stayed like that for a while, until Cheryl finally said, "She's beautiful, isn't she?"

Ally nodded, bracing herself for bad news.

A tear fell from the birth mother's eye. "This is the hardest thing I've ever had to do, but it's for the best."

She stopped, swallowed hard. Her next words barely got out. "Take good care of her."

A blessing.

A prayer answered.

Unable to hold back even more tears, Ally rested her forehead against Cheryl's hand. "I will. I'm going to make Caroline the happiest child in the world."

And she would live up to that promise no matter what it took.

Back in the other hospital room, Jeremiah was trying not to feel like a fifth wheel. The newly arrived Mrs. McCarter and Jessica scurried around, decorating with "Congratulations!" balloons and streamers that Mrs. McCarter had been hiding away until this special day. They'd also brought Ally's prepacked overnight bag.

Both women had been highly disappointed at missing the main action, but they'd recovered quickly.

"How long will it be before we can see the baby?" Jessica asked no one in particular as she tied a balloon to one of the chairs.

"Too long." Mrs. McCarter used her cane to put a stray balloon back into place among its bunch. "A little girl. I can't wait to sew dresses and pajamas for her."

"We'll make her into a regular ol' fashion plate." If Jessica had any doubts about the adoption, she sure wasn't showing it now. In fact, since Ally was allowed to have guests stay overnight in the room, the spots had gone to her aunt and Mrs. McCarter.

Jeremiah wasn't much for fashion talk. And he was sure that he should leave this family alone while they greeted their new member.

"Is anyone up for a snack?" he asked. "I'm headed to the cafeteria."

"Not hungry, but thanks," Jessica said.

Mrs. McCarter grinned at him. "Ditto."

They'd already thanked him profusely for taking care of Ally while they'd been on their way to the hospital. Thank God they hadn't asked just where he'd taken off to with Ally beforehand.

Maybe they knew better.

He walked out of the room, following the small signs that pointed toward the cafeteria. Mrs. McCarter clearly enjoyed having him around, but Jessica didn't seem to care much for him. He couldn't blame her, either, when she'd been in the thick of his social set, hearing every rumor and story that had circulated about him.

Probably Jessica was counting down the minutes until he skedaddled. And he had no reservations about Ally making good on her promise to keep only good influences around her baby.

But he would respect her wishes this time and leave, even if there was still a garbage disposal that needed fixing at her house.

For some reason, that broken disposal hounded Jeremiah as he entered the cafeteria. Ally shouldn't have to handle something like a rogue household appliance when she had so much else on her plate. He should've already gotten it done, anyway.

He grabbed a burger, fries and a soda, and just after he paid for his food, he ran into one of the nurses who'd poked her head into Ally's room sometime along the line. She was a young one, her hair pulled back into thin braids, her eyes big and dark against creamy brown skin.

"How're things going with you?" she asked, holding her tray of salad and bottled water. "The baby's doing well, isn't she?"

"Real well." By now, that burger's aroma was getting to him, just calling out to be eaten.

"I have to say—you and your girlfriend and that baby make for a sight. You're a beautiful bunch."

His...girlfriend.

Again, Jeremiah remembered how he'd felt when they'd been checking Ally in. The staff had first thought that he was with her, a new dad. Some of them evidently were still under that impression.

"I'm not the boyfriend," he said. "I'm..."

What?

The nurse had wrinkled her forehead as he struggled for a word, then said, "...Just a friend."

But that sounded wrong.

"Oh." The nurse seemed embarrassed. "Well, good luck to you and the new mom. She's going to need as many friends as she can get right now."

She went on her way, to a table full of other staff members who were also dressed in scrubs. Jeremiah glanced around, then found his own table.

So the nurse had assumed that he was a significant other. But if people were mistaking him for a loved one just *how* significant had he become?

Even as excitement rolled through him—they had to have seen something obvious between him and Ally—he couldn't eat a bite. He just kept hearing an old voice in his mind.

You'll never change. And it was Nancy's voice, from college. *You are what you are, and I can't set myself up for the day you go back to the old you.*

How could he even think of setting up Ally—*and* Caroline—for that kind of surety? It would be unconscionable when Jeremiah knew damned well that being with Ally and the new baby had only provided him with temporary feelings of constancy and commitment. That he had watched them with that glow around his heart only because it had been a glorious moment that would fade as soon as reality returned.

But as soon as he thought about going back to Texas, his gut bunched.

He'd never been happier than he'd been here, with her. With…them.

He forced himself to eat the burger, then go back to the room. Who knew why when he should've just left altogether.

Maybe it was just the garbage disposal. And, by the time he finished with it, this fantasy of peace and quiet would have worn off, anyway, and he would be ready to go, forgetting about how Ally had broken off a bit of his heart today.

Good and ready.

As he neared her room, he realized that things were quiet. Too quiet. And he found out why soon enough.

Ally was sitting on the bed with Mrs. McCarter, holding Caroline, and Jessica was taking a picture.

After the flash subsided, Ally saw him. Her face lit up, and he knew he'd made the right decision about staying for the time being.

Mrs. McCarter kept her voice low as she said, "Look

who's back! It's photo time, Mr. Barron. Get over here."

"I can't—"

"Nonsense," said the older woman. "You came to the rescue and got Ally here on time for the birth. You're a part of the Gale family story, my boy."

Jessica didn't say much as Jeremiah gave in and sauntered to the bed.

Ally took his hand. "Would you like to hold her?"

"Me?" Jeremiah tried to back off. Newborn babies were delicate and he would be like a bull in a china shop.

"Yes," she said. "You."

Him.

"Maybe another time," he said.

Ally's expression fell, but she didn't push the issue.

Mrs. McCarter saved them all some embarrassment. "Most people are skittish about holding new babies, Jeremiah."

Even as she assured him, he still felt as uncomfortable as could be, a stranger among a family.

And when Jessica snapped another picture, he was sure that his discomfort would be captured for all posterity.

Ally could tell that Jeremiah was treading over pins and needles, even as Jess and Mrs. McCarter videotaped each passing minute.

Soon, they got hungry and decided to go to the cafeteria.

Jess handed off the video camera to Jeremiah. "I'm entrusting you with the job of historian."

As they left, he held up the camera in a kind of semi-grateful salute.

Breathing a sigh that she felt she'd been holding for ages, Ally bent to kiss Caroline, then leaned back on her pillows. Jeremiah noticed that they had on matching wristbands.

Ally saw his gaze on them. "Hospital regulation. They tell me that the only time Caroline will leave the room now is when I'm with her. I guess this is how they check whether or not we belong together."

"You do."

She smiled. "We'll be leaving to do a few tests soon, like one for her hearing. And I'm going to give Caroline her first bath. I'm going to see Cheryl again later, too, but Caroline will be here with Mrs. M and Jess."

It was almost as if she was about to ask if he would still be here as well, but thank God she didn't.

He veered away from the subject. "You ready to get home with her?"

"Oh, yeah," she said. "But I'm supposed to stay the night. Then there's more paperwork and tying up every other loose end."

"Paperwork, like a birth certificate?" He put down the camera on a table, as if knowing that she was done with all the pictures for now, too.

"Yes, Caroline gets one for today, but in about eight to ten months…maybe a year…she'll get an amended one, when the adoption is final. I guess Cheryl evidently asked Michele what I was thinking of naming the baby—" this had just happened today, but Ally was sure that Cheryl had only asked because she wanted Caroline to really be Ally's child right off the bat "—and she decided to have 'Caroline' put on the certificate. So that won't have to be changed. I'll also eventually be listed as the mom."

The dad wouldn't be named though, and Ally tried not to think about that part, tried not to feel so aware of Jeremiah standing by her bed, so near her and Caroline.

"You'll be home soon enough," he said. "And then you'll be off and running."

"Jess said something about a homecoming. Are…" She swallowed. "Are you going to be there for it?"

Jeremiah crossed his arms over his chest.

He was obviously remembering their kiss, the doubts he'd seen in her.

"I'd like you to be there," she said.

He hadn't moved. It was as if a thousand different things were stomping through his head, and not a one of them was settling. Not until he said, "Okay. I can get to my handyman tasks, too."

"How about you take care of that after the cake and ice cream?"

She could see the war in him continuing—how he was getting in deeper by the day and she was only encouraging it.

How had this even happened when, only a short time ago, she'd tried to chase him off?

She nuzzled Caroline, the fuzzy baby cap and soft skin feeling so good.

He watched for a moment, and something clicked in his gaze.

"I'll be there," he said.

She just wished he was talking about more than a party.

Chapter Ten

When Ally brought her baby home for the very first time, she noticed that the roses in the new garden were in full, colorful bloom, as if they were welcoming Caroline with as much verve as everyone else.

It'd been a long day at the hospital, mostly because the nurses had taken Caroline to Cheryl for about an hour, and Ally had felt every second of it like a sharp digging at her chest. Yet, when the staff had brought her baby back to her, it had signaled the end of Cheryl's visits with Caroline alone. Then the birth mother had needed to talk with a state social worker, who'd asked her definitively if this was what she wanted to do.

Cheryl stuck by their agreement, and once she'd signed the paperwork, Ally had held Caroline closely while being discharged from the hospital, walking out of its doors a new mother.

Although Ally was tired, she was energized, too, as

she now took her daughter from room to room in the house. She dwelled in the nursery, which was still in need of some finishing touches, but that wasn't of much consequence, because the baby would pretty much be in Ally's room right now, anyway.

The entire time, she just couldn't get enough of the little faces Caroline made, opening her rosebud of a mouth, opening her eyes as if trying to focus…. Every small gesture thrilled Ally. So did the gift from Jess the baby wore, a darling pink knit cap with a flower.

By the time Ally and Caroline joined Mrs. McCarter and Jess in the dining room, the two women had strewn balloons and party favors all over the place. Also, the oak ranch table was loaded down with ice cream and a cake that read, "Welcome to the world, Caroline!"

The women cooed when they saw the baby. Jess came to take Caroline out of Ally's arms, just as addicted to holding her as anyone. Ally hated to give up her daughter, but she was happy that Jess adored Caroline.

So far, so good, although Ally wondered when her aunt would start reminding her that she'd denied her daughter half of a family.

Idly, she glanced around the room. Even though she'd tried not to be obvious, she'd been hoping Jeremiah would be here already.

Mrs. McCarter noticed. "He'll be coming soon enough."

Jess was running her finger under Caroline's tiny chin, putting the baby to sleep. "I'm glad we have some cake because it'll make the crow I have to eat go down a heck of a lot easier."

Ally exchanged a glance with Mrs. McCarter, and Jess didn't miss it.

"Now, don't go thinking that I've stopped keeping my eye on him," she said. "He just threw me for a loop yesterday when he didn't rocket out of that hospital as soon as Mrs. McCarter and I got there. His willingness to stick around was about the last thing I expected out of a man who's known for making himself scarce when things get serious."

Mrs. McCarter was hovering over Caroline now, too. "He's got a heart." She smiled down at the baby, talking to her in a whispered, playful voice. "Doesn't he?"

"I thought it was another part of his anatomy that defined him," Jess said. "But even I can be wrong."

Okay. Miracles did happen, and that was evident in Jess's new attitude. Still, it was a long way between her realizing that Jeremiah wasn't such a terrible guy to her actually campaigning for Ally to welcome his attentions so that Caroline would have that father Jess believed all children should have.

Ally busied herself by parceling out some paper plates with cute hippos and other assorted pastel creatures on them, as her aunt continued.

"You know what convinced me even more about him though? It was the way he looks at Ally. Boy, what I'd give to have a man give me one of those glances."

Even though Jess left off there, the comment spun out further inside Ally, jogging her heartbeat, sending her skin to a heated flush.

She didn't look at her friends, especially since the reality didn't match Jess's fanciful notions.

"He's going back to Texas, you know," Ally said.

Silence reigned, and Ally was actually thankful when the soft chimes from her front doorbell rang.

It caused a cacophony inside of her, too.

Jeremiah.

Pulse chopping, she went to the foyer, where the massive cedar door was lined by panels of etched glass on the sides. Just before she opened it, she absently tucked a strand of hair behind her ear, then caught what she was doing.

Primping for him.

She breathed out, a trembling sound, but she put herself back together again and opened the door.

And there he was, dressed in the usual Western gear. But that wasn't what threw her off.

It was just that she'd never seen a cowboy holding a baby mobile before.

She felt as if she was composed of a molten substance that somehow kept itself together, molecule by molecule—and somehow she was still standing, although it had to be just a matter of time before she crashed into a puddle at his feet.

As he waited for her to say something, he got a sheepish smile.

"Sorry I'm late," he said. "I got sidetracked when I went out for coffee this morning and saw this on the way."

The mobile was a dreamscape of colors and bright stars. A constellation that told her that he was obviously thinking of Caroline.

And her, too?

"It's beautiful," she said, taking his gift. "But you don't have to keep buying things, Jeremiah."

"I like doing it."

He scraped his boots on the doormat, doffed his hat and then entered. When he drew near, she could smell the clean of his shirt, his skin.

She gave an involuntary shiver, wishing she could just go ahead and actually melt into his arms.

A new awareness had been hanging between them since Caroline had been born, as if they both knew that there couldn't be any more flirtation unless it went somewhere.

There couldn't be any more times when she might throw caution to the wind and give in to him as she'd done at the winery, unless he intended to switch gears in his life, putting his wild ways behind him.

Otherwise, he really would have to go this time, even though Ally had seen the adoring look on his face when he'd first laid eyes on Ally holding Caroline, back at the hospital.

But he hadn't come out here to become a father, she reminded herself.

It felt as if a long, brutal crack split Ally's chest as she brought him to the dining room, where Mrs. Mc-Carter and Jess greeted him. Her aunt was a little reserved, as if she was indeed still keeping that wary eye on Jeremiah.

They had their ice cream and cake while Jess told everyone the details of the night she and Ally had spent in the hospital room with Caroline.

"The girl sleeps like an angel," she said, gazing at the baby, who was now being held by Mrs. McCarter. "I guess karma is recognizing all of Ally's good deeds by bringing her the least fussy child in history."

Mrs. McCarter laughed. "Time will tell."

After they had eaten, cleaned up and surrendered all baby-holding privileges back to Ally, Mrs. McCarter and Jess decided to enjoy the rest of the waning day on the patio, along with a glass of wine or two.

"Jeremiah?" Mrs. McCarter asked, inviting him, as well.

"It's not all play for me," he said, indicating the kitchen with a jerk of his chin. "I've still got work ahead."

Ally stayed quiet. She would've preferred to spend more quality time with him before he left. Handymen were a dime a dozen, and she could get one out here with a phone call, but Jeremiah...?

She had come to realize that he was one of a kind, and she wanted to get to the bottom of him. She wanted to hear everything that she knew he was feeling whenever he looked at her and Caroline, because they wouldn't have any other chances to clear the air once he was gone.

But it was as if he was on a mission as he headed to the kitchen.

Did he think he'd already gotten in too deep and just wanted to cut loose and scram back to the safety of his normal life?

That didn't sit right with Ally. He wasn't happy with the norm. He'd as much as told her that.

So why was he being just as remote as she used to be with him?

She decided to leave him alone for a while, giving Caroline a rest from all the excitement instead. With Mrs. McCarter and Jess on the patio, Ally sat in front of the large fish tank in the living room. Inside the watery haven, the fish swam among tiny models of Old West paraphernalia. The hum of the tank lulled her, just like the low lighting that carried over to Caroline, illuminating her precious face.

Ally stroked her daughter's cheek.

What do you think I should do? she thought to her daughter. *Should I march up to him and take the biggest chance I can imagine by laying everything out?*

But what if she did that and he turned out to be another Marco, who'd backed away from all her plans for a family? What if she was taking a highly charged moment of emotion from yesterday and stretching it into an appealing scenario that featured a man who might have it in him to adore both her and her child?

Maybe she was only projecting that onto Jeremiah. Maybe he really *wasn't* relationship material, just as he kept trying to prove to her, first on the Howards' ranch, then by telling her that story about college….

When she heard a movement behind her, she glanced over to find him, his hands on his hips, girded, as if afraid to approach.

How long had he been standing there?

She nearly turned liquid all over again at the expression he was wearing—that adoring yet confused look that he got whenever he saw Ally and Caroline together.

He must've realized his emotions were written all over him, because he shrugged, then said, "I didn't want to bother you two."

"No bother."

He paused, then jerked his thumb back toward the kitchen. "I'll be making some noise in there."

Really? He'd come out here just to tell her that?

When his gaze dropped to the sweet bundle in Ally's arms again, she couldn't take it anymore.

"Jeremiah," she said. "Come over here."

Cautiously, he did, standing next to her chair.

Ally scooted to the edge of the cushion, then stood, offering her baby to him.

"Now that Mrs. McCarter and Jess aren't here to lavish Caroline with their affections," she said, "why don't you hold her?"

In the gap of time between her question and his response, it seemed to grow more and more apparent that she wasn't just asking him to cuddle with her baby. She was asking him to show her that he wanted more than the life he already had, asking him for a sign—any sign—that there was a chance of him accepting what she knew was inside of him.

He glanced down at Caroline, his heart in his gaze.

Then, as if giving up that heart altogether, he lifted his hands.

"How do I do this?" he asked.

A snag in her throat almost kept her from speaking. "Don't be nervous. Here."

She slid Caroline into his arms, making sure her daughter's neck was supported, making sure he was comfortable with her before she let go.

He seemed stunned that he was actually doing this— holding a baby without messing up somehow. And as he smiled down at Caroline, the baby gazed up at him, taking him in with a wonder so pure and innocent that Ally had to inhale deeply to keep from crying.

Couldn't he see that he *was* meant for this?

"Hey there," he said quietly to Caroline. "You wondering if I'm going to drop you, too?"

"You won't. You're a natural."

When he smiled at her, her world tilted on its foundations. But it was as if it had found the angle where it always should've been before—slightly off-kilter, amazingly right in a way she'd never thought it would be.

Ally led him to sit in the chair she had vacated. She wanted to revel in this sight, to get him to stay beyond the time it would take to fix a garbage disposal.

If only he could see what she saw....

As if to answer that prayer, a flash went off behind her, and Ally turned around to find Jess with her camera.

"I had to get *this* recorded," she said.

After a cursory glance, Jeremiah went back to looking down at Caroline, smiling as he touched her hand with his finger.

Jess leaned over to whisper to Ally. "Do you know how much this picture would be worth on the open market in Texas?"

"Jess..."

"I kid, Al."

With a lingering, amazed glance at Jeremiah, Jess headed toward the long hallway, probably off to powder her nose.

As for Ally, she stayed rooted to the spot, feeling as if everything was blooming for her now.

Jeremiah could've spent the entire night with Caroline nestled in his arms. He'd never felt anything more...

well, satisfying. It was as if a whole new world had opened and it swallowed him right up.

But he'd known he couldn't sit in that chair forever. All too soon, he'd gotten up, giving Caroline back to Ally, who'd eventually settled onto a sofa nearby after bringing him a mug of coffee that had since gone cold.

When he had surrendered Caroline, his arms felt just as cooled as the beverage, as if the warmth had left him.

"No more stalling for me," he said. "That disposal isn't going to fix itself."

"You can come back tomorrow to do it," she whispered, since Caroline was sleeping.

The temptation to keep putting off the task, stretching his time out so he could stay, beckoned him. But then he remembered the moment at the winery when Ally had gotten that doubtful shadow in her gaze—the reminder that he was what he was and she didn't quite trust him to fully become anything else.

Hell, he'd promised himself after Nancy that he wouldn't even try to go against his nature, right? Soon enough, he would be showing his true colors here, anyway, even if they looked to be a tamer shade right now.

His shoulders lost some of their heft. "If you don't mind, I should just get this done."

"So you'll be leaving tomorrow then?"

Was there something in her voice that said she didn't want him to go anywhere?

He resisted the temptation to stick around and try to be different for her, but he knew that, in the end, he would break more than Ally's heart. He would do it to Caroline, too, and he couldn't bear that.

"I think it'd be for the best, Ally."

He didn't explain any further, because she had to know what he meant.

When she only nodded then looked back down at her baby, it was as if he was being dragged under the ground. He'd been half hoping that she would put up an argument, but how many times had she told him that she was going to do right by this child? No way was she going to take a risk on a guy with his track record, especially if he hadn't made any promises to her about mending his wayward habits because he knew it was fruitless.

Better to disappoint her now rather than later, he thought, his pulse a dull thud.

"Do you think," she asked, "the noise from the repair will bother Caroline if I get her to sleep for the night now?"

"How far down that hallway is your room?"

"The last one, pretty far back."

"I don't think it'll be a problem."

This was where he should've been retreating toward that kitchen, but he couldn't bring his feet to move.

"Just one more thing?" she asked.

Anything, he thought, and in a different world with different rules, he might've even been able to provide that for her.

"No matter how late it is," she said, "will you knock on my door before you leave? I'll be waiting up because I'd like to say goodbye."

Had her voice cracked on that last word?

He shouldn't even wonder.

"I'll do that," he said. At least now he would be able to get one last glance at Caroline…and Ally.

Then, as he'd done with every other woman, he would move on.

When he went to the kitchen, he didn't look back this time—not like he had after their second kiss, the one under the stars. She was as good as gone, and making sure of it would make him do something he might regret, like telling her that he wanted to stay.

He had no idea how long it took to fix the disposal, but by the time he was done, Mrs. McCarter had stopped by the kitchen to say good-night, and one glimpse out the window showed him a dark sky studded with stars.

Yet, when he looked at the clock, it wasn't exactly the dead of night. Not late enough to make an excuse to Ally that he had avoided a visit to her room because he feared she might be deep in slumber.

After cleaning himself up, he took a breath, then headed down the length of the hallway. When he got to her door, it loomed before him.

Just get this over with, he thought. *Just knock, say goodbye, then get going.*

He raised his hand to knock, but a baby's cry from inside stopped him.

It was a jarring sound, like a tiny, squalling bird about to fall from its nest and, without thinking, Jeremiah went right into the room.

A dim night-light suffused the Old West decor—the black iron chandelier with candles, the brass-framed bed with mahogany quilting, the dust-bitten photos of sunsets hanging on the walls.

But all he really saw was Caroline's cradle, and he went straight to it.

"Shhh," he said, brushing a finger over her cheek.

She didn't seem to know he existed and just kept crying.

Out of pure instinct, he scooped her up, cradling her, *shhh*ing and rocking her as he made his way over to a couch near the shuttered window.

Thank goodness she quieted down, waving around her bunched fists before opening her mouth in what resembled a yawn—or maybe an attempt to make one last noise—and closing her eyes again.

It was only when he sat down that he noticed Ally sitting on the other end of the couch, her hair mussed, her skin flushed, her gaze sleepy.

"You beat me to it," she said in a gritty voice. "She jolted me out of sleep. I think I was out like a light."

Ally didn't move to take Caroline away from him, although he could see that she was dying to hold her.

When he offered her daughter to her, Ally smiled. "No, you've got her settled. I'd hate to wake her up again. She's had a rough couple of days."

"So have you," he whispered.

"I need to get used to a lack of sleep, unless I luck out and Caroline really does turn out to be one of those relatively low-maintenance babies."

"No female is low maintenance," he said. The light-hearted comment had come out before he'd even thought about it.

But it seemed to be an obvious reminder that he had a lot of experience with women, and Ally leaned her head back against the couch.

"It really has been nice having you here, Jeremiah," she said. "I just wanted you to know that."

"Yeah."

He didn't say anything more, and just as he began to think that she was going to ask him to stay again—and not only because of a garbage disposal—her breathing evened out.

Sleeping. And Jeremiah couldn't help lavishing a gaze over her as he cuddled with the baby, his eyes wide open as he listened to the quiet of the house—a stillness that was punctuated only by the ever-growing beat of his lonely heart.

When Jeremiah awakened, it took him an instant to realize where he was.

By the time he remembered he was in Ally's room, he also noticed that he wasn't holding the baby any longer; Caroline was breathing softly in her cradle. And…

He heard a sigh next to him, just before Ally shifted, leaning against him, her head coming to rest against his shoulder.

Last night filtered back to him: a moment when he'd been fighting sleep… The feel of Ally getting off the couch and taking Caroline from him to transfer her baby to the cradle… A vague recollection of Ally holding a bottle to feed Caroline, then eventually returning to the couch instead of the bed, her body close to his as he reached out to touch her hand right before he drifted off again…

So he hadn't left after all.

Damn it, he should really do it before Ally woke up. Really.

But he liked how she was sleeping right up next to him. He couldn't even remember a recent time when he'd awakened with a woman, since he made it a habit never to linger.

This was good.

Maybe he could just enjoy it for a little while longer?

And he did, leaning his head against hers, running his knuckles over her bare arm, then holding her hand.

He gave himself a half hour, and that was when he told himself that he couldn't do this forever, and if he wanted to make a clean escape, he *would* have to go.

Now.

Heart heavy, he tenderly readjusted Ally so that she was lying down on the couch, her hand against a cheek as she breathed in…out….

Then he went to Caroline's cradle, bending down to kiss her.

Emotion jammed in his chest as he forced himself to walk away.

He opened the door quietly, then closed it behind him….

Only to find that he wasn't the only one in the hallway.

He came face-to-face with Jessica, whose mouth was agape.

Jeremiah looked at her, then looked back at the room.

Oh, hell.

"This isn't what it looks like," he whispered.

He could see the slow boil of anger consuming her. Even so, she kept her voice to an early-morning level.

"It better not be what it looks like," she said.

"I'm serious, Jessica. Ally told me to let her know when I was done working last night, but when I got here, I heard Caroline making a fuss inside. I'm not used to the sounds babies make, so I went right in to see if she was okay and somehow I just…stayed."

At Jessica's widened eyes, Jeremiah added, "There was nothing wrong with Caroline, so don't worry about that. Ally had the situation under control, anyway. It's just that I ended up holding the baby a little longer than I meant to and I fell asleep in there. That's all."

Ally's aunt seemed torn between believing him and doing as everyone else usually did when it came to trusting him—turning their backs.

Then something seemed to bend in her, and she took her digital camera out of her skirt pocket. She must've been carrying it around to capture baby moments when they happened. Maybe she'd even been coming to Ally's room so she could take a picture of Caroline and her first morning waking up in her new home.

She turned on her camera, pressed a button a few times, then showed him the small screen.

On it, he saw a man holding a baby in his arms in front of the glow of a large fish tank. There was such obvious affection on his face that it took Jeremiah a second to realize that he was seeing himself.

"That's how you look at Ally, too," Jessica said. "Like you don't care who sees you acting smitten."

He couldn't tear his gaze away. He seemed like a father if there ever was one.

But, most of all, he looked as if he would never be

the type of dad who would shut his child out, as his own father had. Not ever.

"I can't believe I'm saying this," Jessica whispered, "but all I want for Ally and Caroline is a man to be so in love with them that he looks at them this way forever, as if he's always going to be around and nothing is going to stop him."

It seemed as if she was going to say more—maybe even to tell him about how her dad had taken off once upon a time—but then Jessica put her hand to her mouth and left him standing there.

She'd said Jeremiah was a man—and one who didn't seem the type to abandon.

Was there any going back to his old life now?

He just didn't know anymore.

More baffled and heartsick than ever, he headed for the exit, then his pickup, which he jumped into before he could be lured back inside the house. He drove to his hotel, telling himself he was going to pack.

But when he got a call from his brother Tyler, there was no way Jeremiah would've been able to stay anyway.

"Check your email," Ty said over the phone.

Jeremiah turned on his computer, going online.

What he saw there just proved that he would always be *the* Jeremiah Barron, playboy, no matter what Jessica's picture had shown him this morning.

Chapter Eleven

The headline was from a San Antonio business blog's gossip page, a resource consulted frequently by Jeremiah's contemporaries, whether they admitted it or not.

The Big Bad Wolf Strikes Again! it read.

Underneath it, there was a picture showing Jeremiah in close quarters with Ally back at the Howards' charity ball. He was leaning over to whisper in her ear as she remained the cool, polite, yet distant hostess who'd thwarted him over and over again.

Jeremiah's stomach pitched as he surveyed the short gossip item beneath it, written by the town's biggest anonymous blabbermouth.

It seems as if our cad about town, Jeremiah Barron, has grown bored of his usual prey and decided to switch up his game by homing in on a bigger challenge. My source tells me that the wolf first began circling the lovely and very *upstanding Allison Gale at the annual Red Cross charity event in San Antonio over a month and a half ago. Then, soon afterward, at the Howard family's Help for Children Foundation shindig, he made his big play for Ms. Gale.*

Barron, the son of Eli Barron, who's no stranger to this column (Papa Wolf graced us with San Antonio's most recent great society scandal, recall?) looks to be just as colorful as his father in the future, so tune back in for more on this one....

As Jeremiah just stared at the computer screen, the phone line hummed.

Numbly, he thought that at least the gossipmonger hadn't had any "sources" who cared enough to pursue this story to the hospital, where Ally had walked out with Caroline.

But was it only a matter of time before that happened?

On the other end of the phone, Ty finally said, "Just wanted you to be aware of what that rag was saying, Jer."

"This rag just brought a woman who usually stays out of the dirty spotlight right into it. And it's because of me."

He wanted to strangle this blogger. Strangle himself for doing just what Ally had successfully avoided until he'd put her in his sights.

How could he have forgotten how the real world worked? Had being out here, away from it all, put him in some kind of fantasyland?

The words from the blog lingered. *Just as colorful as his father...*

More than ever, Jeremiah knew that there was no leaving the past behind. Even if he wanted to do it, others weren't going to let him.

Nancy, his college girlfriend, had been right. He couldn't change, not even with the sway of a good woman like Ally.

When he thought of her and Caroline, back at her house, he felt as if he'd lost a piece that he had just fit into himself, like a missing cog that made everything run with the perfection he'd been wishing for.

Tyler's voice took on a note of surprise. "You actually care about what they're saying?"

"This time?" he said. "Yeah."

Ty must've heard the rawness in Jeremiah's tone. The devastating heartbreak of knowing that hope had died, just when he'd discovered it.

"Maybe you should tell me what's going on," Tyler said.

Jeremiah couldn't look at that picture of him and Ally at the Howards' ranch anymore, and he turned away from the laptop screen.

"I'm not sure what's happened," he said.

But that was a line of crap, and even Tyler knew it.

"You went out there," his brother said, "and something big went down, didn't it? And I'm not talking about a land deal. You were going after Allison Gale, but she got to *you*."

All Jeremiah's defensive instincts told him to deny it, and it would've been so easy to do just a week ago.

But now?

Now he was done dodging and weaving.

"She got to me," Jeremiah said. "Her and the baby she adopted."

Tyler listened as Jeremiah spilled everything. The old him might have been flippant about the tale, painting it as just another adventure, a challenge he'd backed out of because there were even bigger ones waiting for him somewhere else. Yet, he couldn't do that now.

"Well," Tyler said in the end. "How about that."

"What?"

"You're in love, you idiot. Or haven't you realized it yet?"

From the soreness in his chest, Jeremiah had known it was something foreign.

But love?

He'd never thought himself capable, just as he'd never thought his father capable.

Yet, he couldn't argue with how much it bruised him to be away from Ally, from the baby…from everything he'd stumbled over out here.

"Knowing that I might not see her again…" Jeremiah said. "I can't stand it."

"And it's not going to get any better. So just get back to her place and work it out."

"You make it sound so simple."

"Believe me—it's not. But if she's worth it, Jer, you'll accept right now that life's never going to go back to the way it was before you fell for her."

"But that's just it." Jeremiah slumped in his chair.

"My life is *always* going to return to the way it was, Ty. Even if I have the best intentions, I can't help myself."

"Next you're going to say you were born to be that way."

Whoa. Hearing Tyler say it made the sentiment sound lame.

But wasn't it?

Had Jeremiah just been using it as an excuse never to put himself out there again, to never risk failing when he tried to improve himself?

Still, he tried to rationalize. "The last thing Ally needs is my kind of trouble. Why would I ever expect her to take on gossip and scandals and all the suspicions she'll have when someone publishes another damned blog entry about how I looked at a socialite cross-eyed? Why should Ally have to take on that load besides everything she's already got?"

"Because she just might love you right back. Does she?"

"I...don't know."

Then he thought about all the glances that had brought about his fall. Thought of how she had asked him to stick around her place, even after he'd seen that doubtful look in her eyes yesterday.

Was she willing to put up with him and hope that he could redeem himself? Had he finally found the one woman strong enough to do that?

Out of the corner of his eye, he could see the gossip column on the computer, seething from the screen like a living creature.

And that was what won out in the end.

Best leave before things got too hot to handle, he thought, shutting the lid of the computer.

Best leave before he made Ally's life, and the baby's, any harder.

When Ally had awakened this morning, she'd found an empty spot next to her on the couch where Jeremiah should've been.

But, although she would've loved waking up to the sight of him, the vision in the cradle nearby assuaged her moment of longing.

"Good morning, sunshine," she whispered to the still-sleeping Caroline. It had obviously been a lot of work to be born.

She left her bedroom, bringing the baby monitor with her, and let Mrs. McCarter, who was just stretching awake in her own room, know that she was going to get ready for the day.

So, as Ally showered, the older woman kept a more than willing eye on Caroline. And, soon enough, everyone, including the baby, was up and about, drawn by the aroma of bacon, eggs, sausage and pancakes from the kitchen, where Jess was cooking away.

When Ally didn't see Jeremiah there, her stomach took a dive. Surely he'd just gone back to his hotel and would be here later, right? She was certain of it, after what had gone on last night, with him staying next to her on the couch, a gentleman through and through. She'd never felt such bliss from simply being held by a man before and, strangely enough, she'd even begun to feel as if she, Jeremiah and Caroline were already a family.

Or at least could be one.

Jess noticed that Ally kept glancing around and, as she took a seat at their table in a nook of the kitchen, she said, "If you're looking for Jeremiah again, he already left. I saw him early this morning."

"Did he say what his plans were?"

"No. But if I were to hazard a guess, I'd say that he'll be back with a truckload of more baby gifts."

See—even Jess wasn't worried.

Content, Ally kissed Caroline and hugged her close before slipping the nipple of a bottle between her baby's lips, just as she was supposed to do every two hours. She'd even woken up last night to feed her baby, and it had given her the opportunity to watch Jeremiah sleep, too.

Who knew that the devilish guy could look like a bit of an angel in that state?

Mrs. McCarter drizzled syrup over her pancakes. "Why don't you just call Jeremiah to see when he'll be by?"

Ally frowned. "I never got his phone number."

She tried not to think that was some kind of bad omen, because it was patently ridiculous. They just hadn't needed to exchange phone numbers yet.

Jess took out her smart phone. "I'll call the hotel and get patched through to his room. Where's he staying?"

"The Sea View in Pismo."

Caroline made a squacking sound as she lost the nipple on the bottle, but Ally guided it right back in.

Jess made quick work out of looking up the hotel,

then asking the clerk to connect her with Jeremiah Barron's room.

She made a puzzled face and said thank-you to the person on the other end of the line, and Ally felt that bad omen niggling at her again.

"What?" she asked Jess as she hung up her phone.

"They said he checked out this morning."

Now the niggle turned into a mini-storm in Ally's stomach. "When he left this house, did he tell you he was planning on checking out, Jess?"

"No." Her aunt's jaw tightened, as if her old opinion of Jeremiah was creeping back up on her.

"He'll be in touch," Mrs. McCarter said, ever the optimist.

But, as breakfast wore on, the air seemed to seep out of the room.

Why did it feel as if something was very wrong with Jeremiah?

Reasons flew around Ally's head. Maybe his dad had needed some immediate attention. Yes, that had to be it. Jeremiah had probably gotten an early-morning message and just hadn't had time to contact her yet....

Then Jess, who'd been pressing the icons on her phone screen, let out a gasp. And when she glanced up at Ally, something told her that all really was *not* well.

"I just got this news link from a friend in San Antonio," her aunt said, handing Mrs. McCarter the phone first. "It might have something to do with why our guest is MIA."

As she kept the phone, the older woman knit her brow before sending a concerned look to Ally.

"Someone had better tell me what's happening," Ally said, trying to remain calm. She held to Caroline, not wanting to let her daughter know that her mother was ruffled.

Slowly, Mrs. McCarter showed Ally the phone screen, where a picture of her and Jeremiah at the Howards' ranch glared back. After Mrs. McCarter scrolled down to highlight the gossip column, Ally read it.

A sick feeling roiled in her stomach.

Had this driven Jeremiah away?

But she knew the reason for his absence had been caused by something more than being featured in a gossip column. He'd probably equated this item with the look he'd seen in her eyes yesterday, when she'd suffered a moment of doubt about who he was and who he could be.

Yet, now he was just gone. He hadn't even stayed to ask if she had it within herself to ignore everything in this column and move on with him. He hadn't thought she cared enough about him to take that chance.

But she *did* care. She'd come to care too much.

She'd fallen in crazy, inexplicable love that, all the same, felt so right.

It seemed as if she was coming apart, and the only thing that kept holding her together was Caroline—the comforting, slight weight of her baby in her arms.

Ally didn't want to think about how Jeremiah had probably told himself that she wouldn't ever believe in him now—especially after the ugly things this column had pointed out. What hurt even more, though, was that he'd obviously given up on *himself,* on all the progress she thought he'd made by being with her.

Jess spoke. "I should've known it. Just when I came around to the jerk, he takes off without a word."

"Jess," Mrs. McCarter said warningly. "Don't jump to conclusions."

"Why shouldn't I? He's just what everyone thought—here today, gone tomorrow. Totally predictable."

"Jess." Now when Mrs. McCarter said it, there was a note of compassion. "He's not like your father. Stop making it sound like he is."

That made Jess clam up right away, and Mrs. Mc-Carter turned to Ally, resting a hand on her arm.

"If I understood anything about Jeremiah, it's that he might've seen this gossip item and he's doing something to keep you out of its sordid business. He might've gotten some kind of heroic notion about leaving before he drags you any further into the muck."

"Does he think this is going to decimate me?" Ally asked, voice shaking as she pointed to the phone and the story.

"I'm sure he does."

Ally shook her head. "I've been through a lot worse, and I've come out of it just fine, too. How can he think this would faze me more than his leaving would?"

There it was. No more keeping it back.

She wanted him here, with her. With them. Always.

"We know what strong stuff you're made of." Mrs. McCarter squeezed her arm. "He'll realize it, too, and he'll call. I'm sure of it."

But Ally wasn't so certain.

Was she worth the effort—the courageous risk—that it would take for him to put his feelings out there, even if he was afraid that she would lose faith in him someday, as the real love of his life had way back in college?

His wounds ran deep, and they wouldn't disappear in the time she and he had been together. They might not even disappear anytime soon....

She gave the phone back to Jess, then glanced down at Caroline, who seemed to have a sad look on her face, her lips pouting, her gaze bewildered.

Don't worry, Ally thought to her daughter. *Mrs. Mc-Carter's always right. He'll call.*

But, after a few days passed and there was still no word from him, Ally wondered if, this time, Mrs. Mc-Carter had been wrong.

Home sweet home, Jeremiah thought bitterly as night fell just outside the lounge windows in the Barron family's mansion on their Texas ranch. Next to him, on the settee, his brother Tyler sat in blue jeans and boots. With his brown hair and green eyes, he resembled their deceased mother more than their father, who reclined in a wingback chair, loosely holding a drink in his hand.

His dad—the stockier, ruddier model for Jeremiah, with his dark blond hair and blue eyes that had been muddied red by drink.

Jeremiah had been fighting off thoughts about that gossip column—and Ally—ever since he'd caught the first plane out of San Luis Obispo a few days ago. He'd kept telling himself that it was easier to be distracted here, in Texas, back in the offices of the Barron Group as well as in this room where Tyler had managed to corner Eli before he went out on the town again.

And he hadn't thought of Ally or the baby for at least

fifteen minutes now, either. He *couldn't* if he intended to function, if he wanted to go on with life and forget what he'd almost done to them by including them in his messes.

But that didn't mean he still didn't feel Ally in the pit of his stomach. In his very core.

Tyler leaned forward on the settee, indicating to Jeremiah that he was ready to start with their dad.

"You're staying in tonight," he said to Eli.

Even Jeremiah knew that this was no way to deal with their father, a baby if there ever was one.

"I'll do what I damned well please," Eli Barron said with a mean stare. "Where's Chet?"

The sudden change of subject made Jeremiah shift position on the settee—so did the punch of his father's preference for his new son. Then again, Dad had known that mentioning his fondness for their new brother might rankle Tyler as well as Jeremiah.

Things really didn't change, did they? Jeremiah had known it when he'd seen that gossip column, and it was doubly so now.

A sense of powerlessness squeezed his head, but wasn't there a lot he could do to fix things? He could call that gossip blogger and set the record straight about Ally's reputation. And he could tell his father just what kind of damage he'd done to all of his sons, and not only recently, either.

But by doing either of those, Jeremiah ran the risk of bringing down even more damage while trying to correct what was already there. By contacting the gossip blogger, he might make the story even bigger than it already was, and that was why he'd refrained so far.

And by letting loose on his dad, Jeremiah just might send his father further over a cliff.

He clenched his hands. Where was the fighter that had always come out in him during adversity? Where the *hell* had he gone?

"Chet," Tyler said, "is on a business project out of state. But you knew that."

Eli rolled his eyes.

That was the final straw for Jeremiah, and he was talking before he could even think better of it.

"Your petulance drove him away, Dad."

There was the fighter—back again.

At least in this case.

Eli wasn't amused. "Aren't you supposed to be chasing some skirt, Jeremiah? I didn't ask you to come back here."

"But I did."

"Lucky me."

God, why had he bothered? Why had he left the best thing he'd ever had going in exchange for this—a life that would never change?

Jeremiah sat there, realizing that everything had *already* changed, even without his permission. His dad had already gone from being just an adulterer to also being a belligerent drunk, and there hadn't been anything to do about it.

And Ally?

As Jeremiah watched Eli down his drink, he became restless, feeling as if the last thing he should be doing was just sitting here....

His father stood, swaying just before he headed out of the room.

Both Tyler and Jeremiah listened to the uneven sound of their father's boot steps fading away.

Ty spoke first. "Progress, wouldn't you say?"

"A startling amount of it."

"I think we need to work on getting Chet here so we can take some drastic steps. There's a treatment facility I've contacted, and they've been giving me advice on how to go about an intervention."

Jeremiah nodded, but Tyler no doubt saw the weariness in him.

"Do I have to intervene with you, too?" his brother asked.

He was talking about Ally now.

"Don't start, Tyler."

A door slammed upstairs, which signaled that Eli had probably turned in for the night. At least he wouldn't be causing any ruckuses outside the house since the staff would be on lookout.

Tyler got to his feet, as if he was done with all the intervening. Then he held up his hand in farewell and left the room.

Jeremiah didn't move a muscle. He just stared at the oil painting of his family above the fireplace mantel: his father, his mother, Tyler, himself.

It was more a memory of a family than anything real.

If his uncle Abe had known what was going on with his brother and his wife, would he have done anything to stop it?

Or did he feel just as helpless as Jeremiah did now?

As he remembered his uncle's last days, Jeremiah heard his phone make a dinging sound, as it did whenever he got a new email. He took it out of his pocket, accessing the message.

He stared at it. Stared some more until his gaze got blurry and heated.

A picture, and it was from Mrs. McCarter.

The photo that Jess had taken of Jeremiah in front of the fish tank with Caroline.

After that, there was more: a photo from the hospital, where Jeremiah had stood next to Ally's bed with Mrs. McCarter, all of them gazing down at the newborn baby. Jeremiah's hand was on Ally's shoulder, a light touch, but he recalled how it had felt as if everything had been in it as he'd made contact with her.

An imprint.

A brand that charred into him even now.

There was also a message that went along with the pictures.

"We saw the blog," it said. "I just thought you'd like a reminder of what you can still have, in spite of a few nasty words from the peanut gallery."

He stared at the images, finally knowing what he had to do. What he *wanted* to do with every breath he took.

He started typing into his phone, creating a draft for a message that he intended to send straight from the heart if Ally would hear it.

Chapter Twelve

Ally had stayed up just about every night, reading her baby books, staring at the ceiling and getting out of bed every two hours to feed Caroline her formula.

As Jess had said before, the baby *was* an angel who didn't fuss much. And Ally wasn't even having nightmares about Cheryl deciding to take Caroline back, because Michele had called yesterday to update Ally, assuring her that she'd heard nothing from the birth mother about reneging on the adoption plan.

No, the reasons Ally had for insomnia had nothing to do with adopting a baby and everything to do with a hollow feeling in her heart.

Jeremiah hadn't contacted her, even if she'd thought, with all her soul, he would. But as the days had passed, she wondered if she'd misspent her faith in him.

Had she misinterpreted who he really was? But how

had she managed to do that when she had been such a good judge of character of other people in the past?

She'd already washed up, putting on a gray skirt and top that covered her a little more, now that autumn was showing up. And while she'd been combing out her hair this morning, she'd seen how tired her eyes seemed. She felt the burn of them, too, but there wasn't a lot of time for napping these days.

She wanted to spend every minute she could with Caroline, like right now, while she played on the bed with her. Whenever the baby did something cute, like making those sweet, happy sounds as she lay on her back, it was more than enough to keep Ally very much awake.

There was a soft knock at her bedroom door.

"Come in," she said.

The door opened to reveal Mrs. McCarter, who was dressed in a long flowered skirt and an oversize blouse. She used her cane to come the rest of the way in, casting a glance at Caroline and smiling.

Then she looked at Ally in a manner that made her think something was going on that Mrs. McCarter wasn't announcing right away.

The old woman couldn't contain a teary smile.

"What's wrong?" Ally asked, already getting off the mattress and going to her friend.

"You ought to ask what's right." Mrs. McCarter limped to the bed, still being cryptic. "Jess and I would like to take Caroline out for a nice, long walk and a picnic, if you don't mind. You'll be needing some privacy."

"Why?" Ally's heart was well on its way to beating right out of her.

Something was definitely going on and Mrs. Mc-Carter was being maddeningly silent about it as she rested her cane against the bed and lifted Caroline into her arms.

Finally, the older woman relented a bit. "Someone's here to see you, Ally."

Everything seemed to go still, like a watch that had stopped ticking, although Ally's pulse took care of marking the missing seconds.

She started getting ideas—hopeful ones. But she didn't dare think they could be true.

Was Jeremiah here?

She didn't have it in her to play it cool, and she sprang off the bed, knowing where he would be if he had come at all.

She ran through the house to the back patio door, and...

There he was, standing by the rose garden he had planted.

Petals bloomed around him as he waited for her on a gravel path, his back to her, his arms crossed. If someone had seen him for the first time, they would never have known that he was a polished businessman, because he was wearing those worked-in boots and blue jeans—clothing that seemed to peel him down to his very essence.

A lone cowboy beneath everything else.

But that cowboy looked as nervous as all get-out, and Ally's chest closed in on itself when she realized that he didn't know how happy she would be to see him.

He was probably standing there struck by the fear that she would tell him to leave again because he'd already taken off like a woo-them-and-leave-them playboy once before.

But her love made her open that patio door and go outside without another wasted second.

When he turned to her, she allowed herself to drop all shields, let him see just how much she'd missed him, even during the short time he'd been gone.

He wouldn't see *any* doubts in her this time.

He dropped his arms to his sides, then walked toward her slowly, as if still not certain about how she was going to respond. And he was holding a phone in his hand, although she wasn't sure why.

"When I drove up," he said, "I saw Mrs. McCarter and Jess taking breakfast out here. She told me that they would give me some time with you."

"I know." But that didn't tell her why he had come back...or why he had gone. "Is everything all right at home?"

She wanted to give him the benefit of the doubt.

"Same as ever." His gaze was searching hers, even from the near distance that separated them. "I'm sorry I left without saying a word. And without calling to tell you the reason for it."

"I thought it was because of your dad—that maybe he needed your attention. Or because of business."

"It wasn't either." He gestured to the phone. "I know you saw that gossip column, Ally."

"Yes, I did." *When* was he going to tell her the reason he was here?

Was she going to have to pull it out of him?

She recalled the devastated look on his face after she'd doubted him once, back at the winery.

He needed to know that she believed he had grown up since college. That he could be any kind of man he wanted to be.

"I didn't believe a word of it, Jeremiah. Not after what we've been through."

When he merely nodded, not saying anything, the doubt inched its way over her skin.

Had he come here to tell her in person that there was no future for them, and that the blog had only reminded him of that?

Then she thought the worst: what if Jeremiah was so scarred inside that he would never be able to bring himself all the way out of his past?

Ally prepared herself to fight for him—the man she wasn't going to let go without a throw-down.

If those pictures that Mrs. McCarter sent Jeremiah had been the catalyst for his return, the reality of Ally standing in front of that patio door was breaking his heart all over again.

She looked so abandoned, with her skirt whispering around her as the morning wind fluttered the gray material, and it drove home that he'd already hurt her by leaving once. What if he poured out his heart to her, only to see that, during his absence, she had thought things over and he had been right to go in the first place?

Just as he reached his lowest point of doubt, she smiled that smile at him, as if she was telling him everything would be okay if he would just take this risk—the one he'd been so bent on tackling when he'd caught a flight out here.

The biggest one he'd ever faced.

With that smile, all his fears fell away from him, just like layers being peeled away until he was stripped to the bone.

He held up the phone he'd been clutching, making sure the screen was on and then offering it to her.

"So you've seen the first gossip column," he said. "But I have a draft for the second one—a message I'd like to send that blogger."

Ally ventured closer, and with every step, Jeremiah's body beat for her, a battlefield of pounding blood and longing. Even being away from her for a few days had made him feel as if his insides were being torn out.

When she took the phone from him, their fingers brushed, and a strike of need hit him hard. But his reaction had nothing to do with lust. Not anymore. Jeremiah needed more from Ally than a notch on his bedpost or a boost to his ego.

He'd never needed anyone like this, and it should've been enough to unman him. Yet, he'd never felt more like a man than in this moment.

Her man, if she would just say yes.

Ally scanned the email on the phone screen. He'd already looked at it so many times that the words seemed embossed in his mind.

Jeremiah Barron here. Tell this to your readers: They can go ahead and let their daughters outside again, because I'm a one-woman man now.

I'll be making an honest man out of myself with Ms. Allison Gale, so the wolf is officially off the prowl.

Ally hadn't glanced up from the phone screen yet, and as she kept reading, his head got light, screaming with the blood that battered the rest of his body.

This was it. Yes or no. She had his life in her hands, and he didn't know what he would do if she gave back that phone and told him that she could never risk the security of her quiet life with her daughter for one that could change at any time if he blew it.

But, when she did look up, her blue-green eyes were bright, as if tears were on their way. "You're telling the columnist that you're off the market?"

Now his pulse was ramming at him, his adrenaline flashing, making it hard to say anything. But he was going to say what she needed to hear if it was the last thing he ever did.

"Ally, I was off the market the moment I saw you across the room that night at the Red Cross event."

She bit her bottom lip, as if to keep back a swell of emotion, and he closed the final gap between them. Then, not caring about anything else, he cupped her face in his hands.

Her skin was so damned soft, and each time he touched it, it felt like a brand-new sensation, lighting his nerve endings on fire.

"I never knew what I was missing until I met you," he said. "I spent too much time looking in the wrong places for the wrong things, and all along, the answer was so damned simple. You even tried to tell me what

I was lacking back at the Howards' ranch, when you saw me with those kids. You knew me better than even I did."

"I knew there was a good man inside who was dying to get out."

She leaned into him, pressing her palm against the back of his hand. He'd never experienced this before—a woman reveling in a mere touch from him. He'd never known he could do that to another person.

As she looked up at him with those beautiful eyes, he got lost—but it was in a good way this time. He was drowning in her, floating….

Becoming.

He bent to her, fixing his mouth to hers. A kiss—one that rearranged everything within him, bringing on a new era. A new Jeremiah.

Someone who had finally found the value he'd been searching for in the last place he'd ever expected.

In her arms.

He whispered against her lips. "I'm never going to let you down, Ally. Never again."

"I know that."

Standing on tiptoe, she wrapped her arms around his neck, bringing him closer, threading her fingers through his hair as she sought more from him, another kiss.

Deeper.

Longer.

His mind spun as he gripped her waist, hardly believing that all he'd had to do was be himself with her. He'd never thought he would be able to accomplish this, but here he was, and the acceptance was making him reel.

When she came up for air, she ran her free hand over the back of his neck, around to the front, where she rested her fingertips over his jawline.

"I love you," she said, every bit of her exposed in her gaze. "And I'm so glad you came back before I had to go after *you*."

"You would've done that?"

She grinned. "I would've found a way."

He was flying now. "I love you, too."

But that wasn't good enough, and he lifted her high above him as she braced herself against his shoulders.

"I love you more than I ever thought possible, Ally Gale."

She laughed, clearly overcome, as he spun her around, down, into his arms again. She clung to him, her chest against his, their hearts beating at each other like they were using a code that Jeremiah was only now able to unravel.

"I've never said that to anyone before," he admitted. "I never thought I'd get the chance."

"I never thought I'd hear you say it. When you left, I thought you were gone for good. But something inside of me knew you were going to come back."

"I wouldn't have been able to leave you behind." He was still holding her against him. "I want to spend every livelong day with you. With Caroline, too."

She closed her eyes, smiling, and a tear leaked out.

"Would you...?" he asked.

"Yes," she said on a breath, opening her eyes.

He laughed. "You know what I'm asking before I've even asked it?"

When she nodded, he wasn't surprised. More than anyone on earth, she knew what he was about.

But he wanted to say what was in his heart anyway.

"I want to be here to see your face when Caroline takes her first step," he said. "I want to see you coming down an aisle in a white dress…the look on your face as I watch my future moving toward me."

She slid down a little farther, her breasts crushed against him even more.

"I want," he said, "to fall in love with you all over again every morning when I wake up."

She slipped the rest of the way down his body, never losing contact with his eyes. Their linked gazes spread flame through him, burning him from the inside out.

With care, he took the phone from her, pressed an icon that allowed for the message to be sent to that blogger.

She took him by the hand, marking the moment that he gave up the old life, coming into this new one.

"Let's move forward right now," she said.

The fire roared in him as she led him to the patio door. In his mind, he heard the echo of how she had used that door to shut him out so many times. But that was when he'd been here for his own selfish ends.

Now he only wanted to make her happy, to see her face glowing as he gave himself over to *her,* too, as he'd never given himself to anyone.

She let him in, and he closed the door behind them. An urgent pressure built in him—anticipation.

An end…and a beginning.

From talking to Mrs. McCarter earlier, Jeremiah knew that he and Ally had the house to themselves, and it seemed like a haven as Ally guided him through the living room, then the long hallway.

They were alone with each other, but they were together, and that was what mattered above all.

Excitement consumed him as they came to her room, but the sight of the empty cradle nudged him.

Ally noticed. "This is our time. We'll have all the rest later."

She'd said it with a hint of shyness, even though she'd been the one to bring him back into her bedroom. But he'd seen how bold she could be when they had been at the winery, and the combination—the mix of goodness with a curious wild streak—stoked him even more.

Tucking a strand of long silver-blond hair behind an ear, Ally bit her lip again, then stepped toward him, initiating the kiss this time.

Barely a touch against his mouth, whisper light, but it was enough to send jags of desire through him.

He didn't need any more encouragement, taking her face between his hands, worshipping her with his touch, his lips, sipping at her with desperate emotion. She pulled at his shirt, just as hungry for him as he was for her.

In fact, she was the one who started to undo his buttons. One, then another.

Air hit his exposed chest, followed by the light sketch of Ally's fingertips as she explored him, parting his shirt even more.

His belly clenched as she went lower, over his ribs, his stomach, down to his belt.

But even though he was dying for her, he wanted to

make this last, because it was their very first time. *His* true first.

He clasped his hands over hers, brought them up, kissed her fingers. She sighed, and that was all it took to lift him to an even higher level of wanting.

Licking flames. Hot spots.

A fire only she could put out.

He unbuttoned her blouse, taking the same care she had shown with him. All the while, she kept her gaze on his, her lashes so thick around those sea-hued irises that it pierced him, her lips parted, her breathing coming faster now.

When he was done, he coaxed back the material, and she did the rest, straightening her arms so that the blouse hushed to the floor.

She stood before him in her bra—white lace against pale skin. A sinful hint of dark pink under the innocent, delicate design.

He used his thumbs to circle her nipples, making them stand out against the lace. Her arousal bit into him, and his jeans started getting tighter.

"My beautiful Ally," he whispered, bending to her, taking one lace-covered nipple between his lips, gently tugging on it. Then he licked it through the material, and she moved with him, groaning a little.

Her pleased sound jabbed at him, and he swirled his tongue over her nub, getting her bra damp. When he looked down, he saw that the pink was darker against the white now, the lace clinging, ramping up his desire even more.

She reached behind her, undoing her bra, allowing it to fall away. Her breasts were small, firm, perfectly round, and he cupped them, bending down to one so he could lavish it with his tongue, taking her in, out.

Clutching at his shoulders, Ally brought him closer, then grabbed at his hair.

"I knew you were going to make me feel this way," she said. "So good…"

He eased her around to the bed, laying her down. Her arms curled above her head, making her breasts fuller.

She was everything—moon, stars, universe—and he had the rest of their lives to explore her, even though he was going to start now.

Tugging down her skirt, he found underwear that matched the pure lace of her bra. He tugged the skirt down farther, exposing her lean thighs, shapely calves, slim ankles.

He slipped off her sandals, then slid his hands back up her leg, raising it just enough so that he could kiss his way over her body.

Her ankles…

Her calves…

Then behind the knee…

She bucked as his lips made contact with that soft spot.

Grinning, he traced the tip of his tongue over the same area, just as lightly.

Just enough to bring her hips off the mattress again.

She was clutching at the quilt now, pulling the material off the corners.

"No one's kissed me there before," she said.

Jeremiah paused. What had her past boyfriends spent

all their time doing with her if not trying to find her sweetest spots?

But he didn't want to think about before—not when he and the woman he loved had a whole lifetime ahead of them.

"Then how about this, too?" he asked.

He turned her over so that she was lying on her stomach, and he planted his lips on the small of her back, dragging his mouth up her spine, concentrating on each bump. Kissing, nipping.

She arched against his lips, and another delighted sound escaped her.

Relishing her, he spent a lot more time testing hidden areas, bringing her to new places merely with his mouth and fingers.

She'd brought a new man out in him, and he was damned sure going to bring a lot more out of her than she'd ever imagined.

Ally had only fantasized what it would be like with Jeremiah, who was so much more experienced. She'd even wondered if he would find her lacking.

But with every sip at her skin, every new erogenous zone discovered, she could see how it pleased him to introduce her to new delights.

And that brought out a straining need in her. A pushing, ticking time bomb that was going to make her explode before this ended.

He had doffed his shirt and footwear, wearing only those jeans now, and she couldn't stop looking at the gorgeous contours of his body: the cut arms and chest, which had a trail of hair that disappeared into his belt line, just begging for her to follow it. The ridges of his abs. The lines of his waist and slim hips.

All of it caused a prickle of desire between her legs. But that wasn't the only thing going on in her awakening body—there was also a wonderful sinking sensation in her belly, a wanting that went beyond the physical. A torrid knowledge that she had been meant to find Jeremiah, just as she'd found so much else this past month.

He was drawing her panties down now, revealing her slowly and gently. And when he had the material all the way off, he took a moment, looking down at her.

The love in his eyes told her everything, but when he spoke, he obviously wasn't afraid to voice what was in his heart anymore.

"Where were you all my life?" he asked with a tender grin.

"Waiting," she said. And she was waiting now, for him to come into her, fill her, complete her.

He rested his hands on her thighs, sweeping his palms up, separating her legs until she was open to him. She gasped at the vulnerable sensation, and when he ran a thumb through the middle of her, she couldn't breathe at all.

She was already primed for him, but as he pressed against her most sensitive spot, her gaze went bleary—star-filled and glittery with a needled craving.

"Jeremiah…" she said.

And he knew exactly what she wanted, too, because she heard the rustle of his jeans coming off, hitting the floor. Felt the mattress shift and creak softly as he climbed onto it.

Then…

Oh, the tip of him, nudging her, stroking up the middle of her folds, then back down.

She rocked up against him, inviting him in.

Done with the teasing, he slid into her, and she sucked in a breath.

Full, so full…

He pushed farther inside, moving with a slick, deliberate rhythm, and she wrapped her legs around his, trying to get even closer to him.

Closer…

Her mind turned into a pool of water. As the calm surface waved outward with gentle ripples, she went fluid, too, her body malleable, all his.

But then it started—a simmer under the surface, a bubbling sensation rolling to the top, and soon, she was boiling, faster, hotter, rising like steam that tumbled over itself, light as air, lifting to—

As she came apart, she felt like a mist that was dissipating. The shape of something ethereal falling into a million molecules and becoming a part of the air.

She felt as free as that air, too, as she moved underneath him, churning, helping him to his own release….

He climaxed with a groan of pure happiness, then one last, laboring strain just before he sank against her, his skin heated, coated with sweat that mingled with her own.

Hot and cool, she thought as he buried his face in her neck. One extreme meeting the other and exploding into something she'd never experienced in all her life.

She held on to one of his arms, feeling the muscle,

the strength. It seemed as if there was so much humidity between them that it would weigh everything down.

But she was on a high, and she could tell that he was, too.

"I think," he said as he tried to catch his breath, "I'd better get you to the altar soon."

"There's a rush?"

He grew serious, brushing back a damp tendril of her hair from her forehead.

"Our kids," he said.

And she understood. He wanted children with her, and he wanted them to know that they would always have security. Marriage would do that.

A commitment from a man who'd never made them before.

Bliss balled up in her chest. She'd been so sure that she wouldn't have the chance to have her own children before it was too late that she'd gone ahead and adopted, and here Jeremiah was, giving her everything she'd ever wanted before she'd made her big decision.

But there was also no doubt a reason that she had been blessed with Caroline, too.

The world worked in mysterious ways.

"You'd better get me to the altar pretty fast then," she said.

"I promise."

And he kissed her, thrilling her from head to toe all over again.

Epilogue

Two Weeks Later

Even though Cheryl hadn't made any claims to the baby—even during a follow-up meeting after the birth, she kept insisting that she wasn't going to—Jeremiah and Ally had legally been required to get her permission to take Caroline on a short trip.

That was because the adoption wasn't official just yet, although it would be within a year. And Jeremiah was counting down every day.

After disembarking at the San Antonio airport from a private jet, courtesy of the Barron Group, the trio rode in a limousine to Florence Ranch on the outskirts of the city, near a little town named Duarte Hill. On the way, Jeremiah kept shaking a baby rattle in front of Caroline as she looked on with wide-eyed wonder from the car seat that faced him.

Next to him, Ally was dressed in a chic, long-sleeved blue dress fit for the cooler weather, plus heels, her light hair falling over her shoulders. Like him, she was tired, but as parents of a newborn, it could've been worse.

Caroline was still a little angel. Then again, even if she had been the type to cry all night, Jeremiah would have insisted to anyone that she had wings.

Although she was the apple of "Daddy's" eye, he and Ally hadn't officially gotten married yet. But back at her California home, Mrs. McCarter and Jess were carrying out all the details for a wedding, which would take place here on the Barron ranch.

When Caroline sneezed—a darling little explosion—he and Ally shared another laugh. He kissed his fiancée.

"I can't wait to get you two all to myself again," he said.

"Me, too, but we'll just enjoy today for what it is."

Trying to conjure a smile, he agreed. With Ally, he was going to try out this family thing with the Barrons and see how it went.

Soon enough, they pulled into the road leading up to the ranch and its "big house."

The Greek Revival mansion reigned at the top of everything: the Texas Hill Country lawns, the pastures and employee cabins farther on down, the swimming hole and meadows that had provided entertainment in Jeremiah's youth.

When they arrived at the big house, Jeremiah didn't even wait for their driver to open his door. He did it himself, holding it for Ally, waiting until she undid the baby's car seat. After she handed it over to him, he looked down at Caroline, who seemed like a little princess with her yellow crocheted hat and pink cheeks.

Then he helped the woman of his dreams out, taking her by the hand, just as spellbound as ever.

He kissed the back of her hand and looked into her eyes, where he saw a love so deep that he was still getting used to the enormity of it.

But he was navigating these new sensations and experiences just as if fate had wanted him to be right here and nowhere else.

When the door to the mansion opened, it yanked Jeremiah out of his reverie with Ally.

Tyler and Zoe were the first outside; they were both dressed in cowpoke gear, a natural fit even though both of them had recently left behind jobs fit for designer suits.

Zoe pulled ahead of Tyler when she saw the baby. As she took the stairs, her stylish, shoulder-length dark brown hair bounced.

"Is this my niece?" she asked, bending right down to fuss over Caroline just as soon as she arrived.

"That's her, all right," Jeremiah said, embracing his brother and quickly introducing both him and Zoe to Ally. "And this is the woman I'm going to marry."

As Tyler and Zoe welcomed her with a warmth that gripped Jeremiah's chest, he trained his gaze back at the mansion's door, where another man had just stepped out.

Chet.

Like Tyler, their new brother was also all cowboy, although he could definitely wear a suit with the best of them. But right now, he had his thumbs hooked into the belt loops of his blue jeans, his Western shirt tucked in. He had their father's stockier build, plus the dark blond hair and blue eyes that Jeremiah had inherited.

For a moment, all of Jeremiah's past misgivings about Chet threatened to overtake him. His new brother was such a reminder of how their father had neglected Jeremiah and lavished all the favor on this son, without Chet having earned it.

But then Jeremiah glanced at his daughter-to-be in her car seat. Then at Ally, who was giving him that smile that never failed to tell him just what he was worth.

Jeremiah turned back to Chet. "You going to say hi to your future niece and sister-in-law, or what?"

It was as if a block of melting ice had been broken between them, and Chet grinned, coming down the stairs. When he got to Jeremiah, they paused, then hugged. But afterward, as if still getting used to having a brother at all, Chet broke away to meet Ally and Caroline.

Ally just kept smiling at Jeremiah. *It'll come,* her gesture seemed to say. *Just hang in there.*

He smiled back, then said to everyone else, "We're hoping that you all can be here for the wedding. A guy needs his best men in attendance."

Tyler slapped him on the back. "You can bank on it."

Chet seemed flabbergasted to have even been asked. He'd been the same way when Tyler had requested that Chet stand up for him at his recent wedding, as well.

Then he grinned. "I'll definitely be here, too."

And that was all Jeremiah could ask, for the time being.

After Zoe had taken Caroline out of the car seat to

hold her in her arms, they all made their way into the house. Before they even got inside, though, Chet got a phone call.

When he glanced at the ID screen, his face lit up.

"Hey, Mina," he said as he answered, lifting his finger to the rest of the group to convey that he would be inside shortly. Then he wandered off, talking to his admin assistant.

As everyone else went inside, Jeremiah watched Chet for a second. It hadn't escaped his notice in the past, before Jeremiah had started doing business remotely from California rather than at the Texas office, that Chet seemed so much more animated whenever he was around Mina. Even so, once when Jeremiah had jokingly asked what was going on, Chet had thrown up his guard and said there was nothing. Just business.

Whatever the case, Jeremiah went into the foyer, highly doubting Chet had known what he'd been talking about. Didn't his brother realize that the only time he seemed on an even emotional keel was when he was around Mina?

But Jeremiah's train of thought came to a screeching halt when the group walked into the study, where his father lingered by the window, as if he'd been watching everyone from this vantage point.

The fringes of his family.

Even more shocking, Jeremiah realized from Eli's tear-streaked face that his father had been crying.

He'd never seen the hard-ass old man break down like this before, and the sight brought him to a standstill. The same went for Tyler as everyone paused at the threshold of the room.

Nearby, flames cast shadows from the fireplace. Above that, the old portrait of their family stayed motionless as Eli spoke.

"I never expected this from you, Jeremiah," his father said. "I never…"

He broke off, lowering his head.

What was his dad talking about?

Then Jeremiah got it. His old man might have had some kind of epiphany while watching his middle child—the worthless, lost cause of the bunch who had finally found his way.

Jeremiah felt Ally's hand on his back, a steadying influence. His everything.

Eli was shaking his head, still looking at the floor. "My first grandchild," he said, "and I didn't feel welcome enough to be out there."

"Dad—" Tyler said.

"No, I need to say this."

Eli wiped a hand over his face, and Jeremiah could tell that he was in between binges, sober for the first time in Lord knew how long.

"I'm going to change," he said. "I swear I will—I didn't have a drop this morning because I knew the baby was coming." He shook his head. "I don't want to be looking through windows at the rest of your lives."

He walked toward his sons and, when he got near enough, grabbed them into a hug. His skin had the sour reminder of alcohol on it, but Jeremiah forgot about that as he returned the embrace, his chest tight.

"I swear," his dad said, "I'm going to change."

The words rang in Jeremiah's ears as they all finally disengaged from each other.

With that said, his father went to Ally, then was introduced to the baby, who was being held by Aunt Zoe.

Jeremiah only watched, not knowing what to make of his father or his promises. Soon, Ally came over to him, leading him away by the arm while still watching Eli as he touched Caroline's hand in affectionate fascination.

"He's going to change," she whispered to Jeremiah. "And you know what inspired that?"

He only nodded. She didn't have to say that when Eli had witnessed Jeremiah out there with his new family, he might have turned a corner.

It was the first time Jeremiah had mattered to his father, and he hoped it would be enough.

All the same, mattering to Ally and Caroline meant just as much, if not more, and he kissed his wife-to-be, thanking her in that one gesture for being there for him.

She kissed him right back, a heaven-filled future in her touch.

* * * * *

Look for Chet Barron's story,
the next installation in
BILLIONAIRE COWBOYS, INC.
Coming soon to Silhouette Special Edition.

COMING NEXT MONTH

Available March 29, 2011

REQUEST YOUR FREE BOOKS!

2 FREE NOVELS PLUS 2 FREE GIFTS!

♥ *Silhouette®*

SPECIAL EDITION
Life, Love and Family!

SSE11

Selene wanted nothing to do with the father of her son,
Alex; but Aristedes had other plans…that included them.

Read on for an sneak peek from
THE SARANTOS SECRET BABY by Olivia Gates,
available April 2011, only from Harlequin Desire.

"You were right to turn my marriage offer down," Aristedes said.

And Selene found her voice at last, found the words that
would not betray the blow he'd dealt her. "Thanks for letting me know. You didn't have to come all the way here,
though. You could have just let it go. I left yesterday with
the understanding that this case is closed."

Before the hot needles behind her eyes could dissolve
into an unforgivable display of stupidity and weakness, she
began to close the door.

The door stopped against an immovable object. His flat palm.

"I can't accept that." His voice was low, leashed.

What did her tormentor mean now? Was he ending one
game only to start another?

She raised eyes as bruised as her self-respect to his,
found nothing there but solemnity and determination.

Before she could voice her confusion, he elaborated. "I
never let anything go unless I'm certain it's unworkable. I
realize I made you an unworkable offer, and that's why I'm
withdrawing it. I'm here to offer something else. A work-
ability study."

She leaned against the door, thankful for its support and
partial shield. "Your son and I are not a business venture
you can test for feasibility."

His gaze grew deeper, made her feel as if he was trying
to delve into her mind, take control of it. "It's actually the

other way around. I'm the one who would be tested."

She shook her head. "Why bother? I know—and *you* know—you're not workable. Not with me."

His spectacular eyebrows lowered over eyes she felt were emitting silver hypnosis. "You're right again. Neither you nor I have any reason to believe that isn't the truth. The only truth. It might be best for both you and Alex to never hear from me again, to forget I exist. But then again, maybe not. I'm only asking for the chance for both of us to find out for certain. You believe I'm unworkable in any personal relationship. I've lived my life based on that belief about myself. I never really had reason to question it. But I have one now. In fact, I have two."

Find out what happens in
THE SARANTOS SECRET BABY by Olivia Gates,
available April 2011, only from Harlequin Desire.

SPECIAL EDITION

Life, Love, Family and Top Authors!

In April, Harlequin Special Edition features
four *USA TODAY* bestselling authors!

FORTUNE'S JUST DESSERTS
by *MARIE FERRARELLA*

Follow the latest drama featuring the ever-powerful
and passionate Fortune family.

YOURS, MINE & OURS
by *JENNIFER GREEN*

Life can't get any more chaotic for Amanda Scott.
Divorced and a single mom, Amanda had given up on
the knight-in-shining-armor fairy tale until a friendship
with Mike becomes something a little more....

THE BRIDE PLAN (*SECOND-CHANCE BRIDAL* MINISERIES)
by *KASEY MICHAELS*

Finding love and second chances for others is
second nature for bridal-shop owner Chessie.
But will *she* finally get her second chance?

THE RANCHER'S DANCE
by *ALLISON LEIGH*

Return to the Double C Ranch this month—where love, loss
and new beginnings set the stage for Allison Leigh's latest title.

Look for these titles and others in April 2011
from Harlequin Special Edition, wherever books are sold.

Harlequin®

A *Romance* FOR EVERY MOOD™

www.eHarlequin.com

SEUSA0411

PRESENTING...THE SEVENTH ANNUAL
MORE THAN WORDS™ ANTHOLOGY

Five bestselling authors
Five real-life heroines

This year's Harlequin
More Than Words award
recipients have changed lives,
one good deed at a time. To
celebrate these real-life heroines,
some of Harlequin's most
acclaimed authors have honored
the winners by writing stories
inspired by these dedicated
women. Within the pages
of *More Than Words Volume 7*,
you will find novellas written
by Carly Phillips, Donna Hill
and Jill Shalvis—and online at
www.HarlequinMoreThanWords.com
you can also access stories by
Pamela Morsi and Meryl Sawyer.

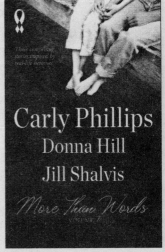

Coming soon in print and online!

Visit
www.HarlequinMoreThanWords.com
to access your FREE ebooks and to nominate
a real-life heroine in your community.

Proceeds from the sale of this book will be
reinvested in Harlequin's charitable initiatives.

MTWV7763CS